Athena's Revenge

A Novel

Graham Duncanson

Chapter 1

I never knew my father. He was killed on the 10th of November 1918 by a German sniper's bullet. It was tragic as he had survived over four years of war. He was 48 years old and had risen to the rank of General by his bravery and courage. My mother was only eighteen when they married in the summer of 1914. She claimed that she was frightened of my father's hairy legs on their wedding night. I found this very hard to believe as, not only was she a very formidable woman, but also it seems likely that my eldest brother, Hector was conceived on their wedding night. I am not sure whether I loved her. I certainly admired her. She brought up three children on her own as she never remarried.

I think my mother and I were destined to fight. She was devoted to both Hector and Aeneas my other brother. They had been named by my father who was keen on ancient mythology. They were Trojans. He had also told my mother that if they had a daughter she was to be named after the Greek Goddess, Athena. I was therefore destined to be on the opposite side to my two brothers for whom I had great affection. They were never aware of this and in fact were hateful to me. I would like to think that this family battle, where I was constantly outnumbered was the making of my strong character. In fact, it is more likely that I am by nature confrontational.

My father was Marquess Huntly and so was by birth 'The Cock of the North'. His regiment was The Gordon Highlanders. Hector joined the regiment in 1932 as a Second Lieutenant. A year later, Aeneas, because of connections on my grandmother's side joined the Royal Norfolk's, also as a Second Lieutenant. They both were experienced soldiers by the start of The Second

World War. I returned to Scotland when I was twenty years old and was determined to fight. I had been sent three years earlier by my mother to Germany to finish my education. I was never sure why, as I only achieved poor academic results at school in England. However, I became fluent in French and German, and excelled at skiing and mountaineering. I saw first-hand, not only the horrific behaviour of the Nazi's to the Jews, but also the debauchery and sexual depravity of their leaders which was fuelled by drugs and alcohol.

My mother thought that I should become a nurse to help the war effort. This did not suit my bellicose ambitions and I became a driver at Bletchley Park. I felt no shame using my aristocratic background to secure the job. I was Lady Athena by birth. As a teenage girl my grandmother taught me the mantra of, 'if you have got good looks flaunt them'. I am sure she did not mean me to seduce the good-looking stable boy, but he had gentle hands from taming young foals, and so I was happy to let him work his magic on me.

I was out celebrating the Miracle of Dunkirk with two of my rather nobby friends at the 'Swan in Bletchley' on the 5th June 1940 when I was called by the barmaid to the phone. It was my mother who certainly was not celebrating. She was furious. My eldest brother Hector had arrived home to announce that he had been promoted to staff rank, which I knew meant that he was now a brigadier. According to my mother, my other brother Aeneas was missing in France and had not been evacuated. What had caused my mother to blow her top was that Hector said he could do nothing about it. She said in a very controlled voice which I knew always meant big-time trouble, "Athena, Hector is now the bloody 'Cock of the North', and he says he can't do anything. You must get over to France and bring Aeneas home."

I replied, "I will leave immediately."

That had the desired effect as she answered in a normal voice, "Good."

I was sure she now was returning to her dinner party as the phone went dead. What the devil should I do? I am not the sharpest tool in the shed, but I knew now was not the time to cross my mother or to be indecisive. I went back to Lydia and Margaret in the bar, "Girls we have a top-secret mission. We need to rescue my brother from France. It is vital for the war effort." Lydia and Margaret are great party girls. They also love adventures. They necked their drinks. Lydia knew that James, the head driver at Bletchley Park, had the hots for her. She saw him at the other end of the bar. She went up to him and managed to persuade him to let her borrow the staff car which was parked outside the pub. The three of us left without delay. I wanted to return to our digs to change, however I knew mother had rung them to find out my whereabouts, so I thought it was best for me to depart and at least show that I was attempting the impossible task. We had to proceed with caution through London because of the blackout. Mercifully the moon came up which helped Lydia to increase our speed through Kent to Dover.

It was after 2.00 am before we reached the docks. The miracle of Dunkirk was over except of course to many like my brother Aeneas. There were plenty of boats for me to choose from. I choose a small motor cruiser with an inboard diesel engine. It was full up with fuel. The owners had been very careless as they had left the keys in the most obvious place, on a ledge over the door. There were some warm clothes in the cabin which was helpful as my pub going kit was totally unsuitable. Also, there was an added bonus of plenty of provisions and water. It was ideal.

I could tell that Lydia and Margaret in the cold on-coming dawn were not happy to steal a boat. I wasn't either but stealing or facing my irate mother left me with absolutely no choice. They had never met my mother, so with some reluctance I suggested that they returned to Bletchley Park and then they would be entirely blame free. If they got going, they would not even be late for their work shifts. So, with hugs they left. Little did they realise that I planned to set off as soon as there was even a glimmer of dawn. I was not concerned with the Germans. My worry was that I would be stopped by The Royal Navy.

I started the engine. I realised how lucky I had been, getting familiar with boats in Scotland, when I was a girl and in Europe on my grand tour when I was 'coming out'. I smiled. I had learnt to loath that expression. The air was still and so casting off was easy, as was controlling the boat. I might have been a thief, but I was not a vandal. I did not want to damage it. As I set my course for Dunkirk, I felt liberated. I was not just placating my mother. I was off on an adventure. I was off to fight. It had always annoyed me that girls were not allowed to fight. I was fond of my brother Aeneas. Heavens knows how I was going to find him. I thought it was a good omen that the boat was called 'Dido'. My time in our library at home had taught me well. I knew that Aeneas when he was on his way to found Rome had had a fling with a queen in North Africa called 'Dido'. She rather stupidly had thrown herself on a pyre when he left her. That was another thing that annoyed me, the women in Greek and Roman mythology were never that bright. I wondered if my father was trying to tell me something. Perhaps his death in 1918 was merciful. Maybe he was not looking forward to returning to my mother and cold wet Scotland.

More by luck than judgement my timing was impeccable. The dawn was up but no one was on the French beach. The tide was in. I managed to gently bring 'Dido' head on up the beach near to a groyne. I could safely leave her without any worries that she would get damaged unless a storm brew up. Obviously, she might be found by the Germans, but I knew there was miles of sandy coastline and I hoped they had other things on their minds.

I set off with a shoulder bag containing some water, biscuits, and apples. I had a six mile walk northwards to reach Dunkirk. I had been walking for about twenty minutes and the town just came into view. I thought I was a bit exposed and so I went into the dunes. It was much harder going, and I slowed up, but I thought that I was less likely to get seen by the Germans. I had not seen any aircraft, neither friend nor foe. It was strange that there were no people. Then I heard male voices. I was near to a large hill in the sand overlooking a dell in the dunes. I hid myself. It was a group of ten British POWs all with their hands tied, being pushed along by three Germans. They were wearing black SS uniforms. All three of them were officers. To my horror the POWs included Aeneas. He like all the POWs looked in a dreadful state. They were filthy and their faces were pinched and gaunt. They were stopped by a German command in the dell. Then with just a nod from the senior officer the other two Germans mowed them down with their submachine guns. The Germans were well drilled. They slapped in fresh magazines.

There had been nothing that I could have done but to remain hidden. However, then I got my chance. The senior officer ordered them to check that all the POWs were dead. They laid down their weapons and set about their task while the senior man casually lit himself a cigarette. I crept forward and grabbed one of the guns. The man turned but he was not quick enough. I killed him with two rounds before turning the gun and killing the other two Germans. I was in a frenzy, but I soon calmed down and made sure that the three Germans were dead. Then I walked to my brother he like the others was dead. With a great sadness I collected the dog tags of the other nine. I knew I would just have to leave their bodies, but I was determined to bring Aeneas home. I took one of the German pistols but left the other weapons. I then managed to hoist my brother's body across my shoulders. I set off back to boat along the beach. I did not care about being seen. It was the worse walk of my life. The horror of what I was doing gripped me, but I laboured on. I am sure if Aeneas had been his normal weight that I would not have managed it, but he had obviously been starved and he was dehydrated. It still was very hard work. I did not dare to stop as I thought that I would never get him back on to my shoulders again.

At last, I reached the 'Dido'. I managed to get him into the cabin, and I covered him with a blanket. Then I just had to wait for the tide which had already turned, to come in again. I hid in the dunes, but no one came. Eventually the water level rose and with some considerable effort, I pushed the boat properly into the water. Mercifully the engine started first time and I backed out into deeper water before turning for home. I was now very tired but at least it was not yet dark and so I made good headway. There was considerable activity in Dover harbour. I was surprised that 'Dido's' berth was still empty. I went in stern first to moor her has she had been before I had stolen her. I was just tying her up when there were shouts, two policemen were running towards me followed by a very irate older man.

I stood defiant, waiting for them. The conversation would have been humorous had we not been in such tragic circumstances. The older of the policeman was a sergeant. He demanded, "I am arresting you for stealing a boat."

I replied, "I have not stolen a boat, Sergeant. However, I have stolen some diesel which I am happy to replace."

The sergeant was now slightly confused and to bolster his and his constable's confidence he added, "That's as maybe. Constable, take this young lady back to the station."

I, in a very calm sad voice said, "Sergeant, in that boat you will find the body of Lieutenant Sir Aeneas Huntley, my brother who was murdered as a POW by the German SS in France, this morning. I witnessed the murder and would be happy to come to your station to make a statement." I turned to the man, "I'm extremely sorry for borrowing your boat without permission. If you could tell me the likely amount of diesel that I have used in the five-hour return crossing this morning, I will reimburse you right away. I would be grateful if my brother's body could remain on board while I organise an undertaker."

The man was much quicker witted that the sergeant, "I am so sorry for your loss. I am Captain Reginal Williams, RN retired. My house is only two hundred yards away. Please return with me so that you can use my telephone." He turned to the Sergeant, "Sergeant I am in your debt. I formally drop any charges regarding this young lady and my boat. I would be extremely grateful if you could leave your constable to await the arrival of an undertaker and you in turn could accompany us back to my house for some refreshment."

I held out my hand, "I am Athena Huntley." There was a general shaking of hands and the three of us repaired to the captain's beautiful sea-facing house. We left the constable, feeling very important, to stand on guard.

The captain took us around to the back of the house. As soon as I entered, I realised that he lived alone. I was intrigued as I had found women's clothes on the boat. In fact, I felt guilty as I had got some of them on. He ushered us into the tidy kitchen and put on the kettle. He suggested to the sergeant that he took a seat at the kitchen table. Then he ushered me though to use the telephone which was in his office. He excused himself to go and make the tea. I took a deep breath and rang my mother, "Mother, I have got dreadful news. Aeneas has been killed in France." This evoked, "How do you know?"

I answered, "I arrived in the dunes when the SS brought ten British POWs out of Dunkirk. They were all officers. They mowed them down. There was nothing I could do."

For once my mother was sympathetic, "Well at least you were there. You did your best."

"I'm so sorry mother. I rather lost it. The three officers were rather un-German and not well trained. They weren't paying attention. I grabbed their gun and shot them all. I brought Aeneas's body back across the channel."

There was a catch in her voice, "All I can say, is well done. I have been very hard on you all your life. You have done just what

7

I would have wanted to have done myself. I will organise everything up here for the funeral. Can you organise a local undertaker to bring Aeneas back to Scotland?"

I replied, "I will get to it immediately. I am ringing from a retired naval captain's house."

Always abrupt, "What's his name?"

I replied, "Captain Reginald Williams."

There is a slight pause, "I was at school with his wife Barbara. She was a Miss McVie then. Sadly, she died of cancer in her forties. I think they had a daughter, but I forget her name. Take care, Athena."

Then I cried. My mother had never told me to take care before. I came back into the kitchen. They both could see that I had been crying. The captain, to hide his embarrassment said, "How do you take your tea?" I sniffled, "Just milk, I'm sorry for breaking down. Tea is just what I need. Thank you."

I took my tea and sat down, "I'm sorry captain about the loss of your wife. She was at school with my mother."

He answered, "How amazing it is a very small world. I still miss her after more than ten years. It is strange as with me being in the navy we spent very little time together. My daughter Helen would be about your age. She works in London. We are very close. She comes down as often as she can."

I was obviously in a state of shock because I started crying again, "I am so sorry I have stolen her clothes. I thought that they might fool the Germans into thinking that I was French."

Reginald put his arm around my shoulders, "You mustn't worry about that. Why don't you sit at my desk in the sitting room and write a report for The Sergeant. I will get on to the undertaker in Dover. I met him by chance only a week or so ago. He was very kind to me when my wife, Barbara, died."

He was a clever man. He knew that he needed to get me busy with a new purpose. I did as he suggested. The Sergeant came with me. He was used to taking statements and so I just dictated

8

my report. I started my tale from my departure from Dover. It was not difficult as it all was so fresh in my mind.

The Sergeant left and said that he would return to the police station, and I could contact him there if he could be of any further assistance. Reginal kindly took me upstairs to his daughter's room and showed me her bathroom. He found some clean towels and suggested that I had a bath and then put on any of his daughter's clothes which I thought would be appropriate. He was so kind. I wept again but the bath rejuvenated me. I did not weep after that. I found a black dress.

When I came down, I found that he had changed into a black suit. He asked, "Would you like me to come with you to your home in Scotland. It is a long way, and we could share the driving."

I answered, "That would be marvellous. I was dreading riding in the hearse."

As it was, it was not a hearse but an army ambulance. The undertaker had been very sensible. I suspected he did not relish driving at a sedate pace all the way up the Great North Road. Reginald and I let them get started on their journey and then we overtook them on the A2 and proceeded with speed to the Woolwich Ferry across the Thames so that we could by-pass London. Coming through Kent we talked about our families and of course it was not long before we started talking about the war. I soon realised that we were kindred spirits. We both wanted to do more. Reginald who I now called Reg was frustrated that because of his age he could not use his skills in defeating the Nazis. I was the same. I was frustrated that I, as a girl, or now I was really a woman, could not use my courage and skill to kill the Nazis. My father had been killed by a sniper who could have been a woman although I thought that was unlikely. Why could not I become a killing machine? I suppose it was vengeance. I knew that revenge was a food best eaten when cold.

I was driving, Reg had dropped off to sleep. I was trying to get my thoughts together as I was driving at some considerable speed just north of Newark. Reg woke and asked, "A penny for them." Without a thought I replied, "I was trying to see how you and I could be an effective team in winning this war. At the moment it looks an uphill struggle. However, with Churchill at the helm at least now I feel we have a chance. Dunkirk was brilliant but it was a rear-guard action. I can't think how we can get the war effort on to the front foot."

I turned to glance at him. He was smiling. I asked, "Why are you smiling?"

He laughed, "I'm just pleased that I am included in your team. Until I met you, I had rather considered myself as being on the scrapheap."

I replied, "You do talk a lot of tommy rot. Think of my mother being the Admiralty. You have just received your posting."

He asked, "Have you received yours?"

I answered, "Of course, I am your First Lieutenant."

He laughed, "On our way through Edinburgh, you had better send out the press gangs to get us some crew."

I replied, "I don't think that will be necessary immediately. Initially I was planning on you to send me out on a one-woman sniping mission."

He asked, "Will your mother approve?"

I answered, "Strangely enough I think she will understand. My brother Hector certainly won't, so we had better keep him in the dark."

Reg stroked his chin, "That is a shame as I think you said he is now a brigadier. He might have been useful."

I nodded, "You are probably right, but I somehow think that he will think killing senior Nazis is not sticking to the Queensbury rules and it is punching below the belt. How would you justify my proposal?"

He replied, "I think if we were having this conversation in October 1805 when we were bearing down on the French fleet off Trafalgar, I would have agreed with Lord Nelson that positioning snipers in the rigging to kill the enemy's officers was not to be condoned. However, it was a sniper who was his downfall, so I will now run with your plan. Maybe we should restrict our targets to the SS and the Gestapo."

I nodded my head once again in agreement and added, "We will somehow have to disguise our actions to prevent the Germans considering taking reprisals on the unarmed populous."

We were both hungry and so we stopped at the smart hotel at Scotch Corner for a late supper after filling up with petrol. I was dreading the rest of the journey as I was bone tired. The food did revive me. I was grateful to Reg at midnight as he then took over and I slept on the back seat. He woke me at dawn with the beautiful view of The Firth of Forth. There was no traffic at that hour and so there was no delay as we crossed the river on the ferry under the massive railway bridge. I was surprised as when I looked back, there was an army ambulance drawing up. I guessed it contained my brother. They had done very well. I was relieved that we would arrive at home before them. It would be a difficult time for my mother. I had detected a change in our relationship. I think she would want my presence although she probably would not admit it to me, or even to herself.

We arrived at my home in Aberdeenshire to chaos. It was not a real shambles. If one was being kind, one might term it organised chaos. Mother had moved out to the Lodge House. Our massive stately home had been taken over by the army as a hospital. Naturally they had not anticipated Dunkirk. There were lines of ambulances waiting to discharge the wounded soldiers.

We were greeted by my mother who I introduced to Reg. Mother insisted on calling him Reginald. However, she was very welcoming and thanked him for his assistance. Then she sent us back to the Lodge House to have some refreshments and more importantly to alert Victor the old gate keeper to make sure that the ambulance containing my brother's body was diverted to the undertaker's funeral parlour. It would lie there for five days before the small family funeral. We had only finished our snack when the ambulance arrived, and I heard Victor giving instructions to the driver. I breathed a sigh of relief. My mission was completed. Suddenly I felt a crushing sadness. My brother was dead. I wept and felt Reg put his arm around my shoulders.

I sniffled, "I will get a grip on myself in a second. I am just over tired from the journey." He wisely said nothing but continued to support me. I took a deep breath, "I think I will have a lie down. I can't remember the lay out of this house. It seems strange not to go to my own room in the big house. Do you want to come with me and find a room?"

He chuckled, "I think we ought to find two rooms?"

I was smiling again, "Yes that probably would be best." We both must have been tired as we slept right through until the following morning. Mother was very understanding. She did not find me any chores but suggested that I took Reginal for a long walk and showed him the area. It was interesting as now I saw some of mother's good qualities rather than her annoying traits. She had specifically said the area and yet I knew she actually meant the estate which of course now belonged to Hector. My mother did not need to show off. I realised then that she never did. She was the daughter of an Earl and so like me was a Lady in her own right. She was not a snob. I realised that in fact she was a good role model.

So, following her lead, my behaviour was exemplary throughout the days leading up to the funeral and on the day itself. It was good training for the years to come. I would be living behind enemy lines. I would never be able to let my guard down.

Reg and I had a leisurely drive down south. He dropped me off at Bletchley Park. I had to go through a full debrief. My immediate superiors were furious, mainly because I could have been captured and then would have revealed intelligence under torture. I was eventually shown into an unmarked room in Whitehall. It was an austere office. The man sitting behind the desk was like a living corpse. His face had been very badly burnt. He greeted me with, "I was sorry to hear about your brother. I have read his file. Men like him destined for high rank will be sorely missed. The Nazis are evil, sadly they are not fools. I have checked on the other nine British officers. They were all good men. I am sure they were not picked randomly. You did well by bringing their dog tags home. Not only does that help their relatives to seek closure of their grief, but also, more importantly for me it gives me insight into the thoughts of the SS command."

This was so different to all the other officers who had debriefed me. I had been looking at him intently. He was very ugly, but his eyes showed compassion. I was bold. I asked, "Were you burnt in action?" He did not hesitate, "Yes, I was on a destroyer HMS Shark. Reg and I shared a life raft after it had been sunk in The Battle of Jutland. He said I would like you. Normally I hate talking to young ladies. I don't blame them for looking away. You are very different. Your beautiful eyes have never left mine. I want you to go on a gruelling physical and mental training course up in the highlands of Scotland near Ben Nevis which has recently been started on pacific orders from The Prime Minister. Then I will be in a better position to find the correct job for you. Let's hope you are aptly named. I think Athena was not only the goddess of war but also of wisdom. Good luck I will see you in this office in six weeks. He got up and held out his hand. I disregarded it and leant forward and kissed him on the cheek. His response was, "I predict that you are going to be more trouble than a box full of frogs, not only to me, but also to the enemy".

I was smiling as I left his office. His middle-aged PA handed me my instructions saying report back here on the 1st of August.

Chapter 2

I was soon on my way back to Scotland. This time on the train. I had plenty of time to read all my instructions. I had been given a naval rank of Lieutenant. I was therefore quite a senior Wren. I knew that would not count for much on the course ahead. It was a hundred percent worse that I could possibly imagine. I was hit, kicked, stripped naked and thrown from some height into a freezing cold loch. All the time my so-called instructors had no names and were clad in balaclavas, so I never saw their faces. They were in the main silent, but I soon learnt their body language. They ground me down with lack of sleep and by humiliating me, they took away myself respect. They made me fire a rifle lying naked in a bed of nettles. Heavens knows whether I hit the target let alone got a bull's eye. I just set my sights on staying alive.

The worst was when they took me up in a light aircraft. My head was covered by a sack I was dressed in fatigues and walking boots. Something was strapped to my back with a lot of fumbling in my groin. These straps were tightened further in the small plane. I just hoped that it was a parachute. I was relieved that I could still hope. There was obviously no door as the wind blew in. Then I felt them tying my ankles together with a strap. No one said a word to me. I was manhandled to the door and then like a bag of rubbish they threw me out. My hands and arms were free I tore off the hood and frantically searched for a rip cord. There wasn't one. My tired terrified brain was not completely dead. I realised that I must be on a static line as sudden there was crack, and my parachute opened. I reached above me and found the toggles so that I had some control. In the distance I saw a smoking bonfire. I knew I must turn into the wind. The ground rushed towards me. Thump. I had my breath knocked out of me. I am not heavy. Mercifully I did not seem to be crippled I was just winded. The strap around my ankles had stopped me breaking a leg. It seemed like an age before I stated breathing as my body had been doubled up in spasm.

The light was fading as it was evening. I got one glimpse of the setting sun. I knew then which was west. What I did not know was whether to go east or west. In fact, I had not a clue where I was except, I was in the heather, and hills were all around me. I fixed a hill in my mind and decided to journey west.

I have never feared the dark and have got good night vision. I kept that same hill that I had seen in my vision in my sights even in the gloom. I had had the sense to wrap up my parachute into a bundle and secure it across my back with the strap which had secured my legs. They had taken my watch, so I did not know the time. I was exhausted and as soon as I stopped walking, I was cold. I found a small area of grass in the heather, rolled myself up in the parachute and slept. I woke cold, hungry, and thirsty at dawn. I could still see my hill. It took every bit of my spirit to set off walking again.

I reached a stream and had a good drink. I stripped off my fatigues so that I could have a crap and a pee. I was just brave enough to wash myself. Now I was indecisive. Should I follow the stream in the direction of the water. Then I would always have some water. I decided against this as the course of the stream meandered and it would be hard going. So, I drank as much water as I could and continued in the direction of my hill in the west. The sun rose behind me. I stumbled along but at least this movement stopped me freezing to death,

I tried to be positive. I was a Scot. I was used to this climate. It was often cold in July. Lack of food was my problem. I disturbed a grouse. I ate her four small eggs. They nearly made me vomit, but they helped to keep me going. It was a grey day and soon it rained. It was not serious rain. It was little more than misty drizzle which we called 'spit in the wee' when we were kids. I pretended that it was better than warm sun. I became more and more miserable. I just kept going. I reckoned that I had been on the move for eighteen hours as it was beginning to get dark when I came to a road. This lifted my spirit, and I headed downhill.

Then I heard a vehicle. It sounded like a small lorry. My indecision was worse because I was so tired. Should I hide or should I try to get a lift. It was coming up hill and I could see it was an army lorry. I was too late to hide. I stood in the middle of the road.

The lorry was full of soldiers. I recognised that the man who got down from the cab was an officer. Not by his face, because he was wearing a balaclava, but by his walk. I was no longer indecisive. I flew at him trying to scratch his eyes out and tried to bring my knee up in his groin.

He just punched me in the stomach and laughed. I doubled over winded. I heard him say to his men, "Well she has found us. At least we won't have to spend the night with the dogs looking for her."

Then he got me up and put my head between my knees and I started breathing again. I spat out, "You are a total bastard."

"You may forgive me one day. Wild cats like you don't sulk. You have done exceptionally well."

He shouted, "Load up, we will return to base."

He helped me to get into the cab. I was too weak to resist. I felt like murdering him. I thought that I would be taken back to their base where I had been abused for the last few weeks but mercifully that did not happen. We stopped in a layby on a lonely road, and I was helped out of the cab by the officer. All the soldiers in the back got out and formed up in a line. They still were wearing their balaclavas. It was quite bizarre. The officer shook me by the hand, "I understand that you will be working alone Mam. However never forget we will all be thinking about you. It was probably hard for you to receive such treatment. I am not alone in saying that it was hard for us as well. We all wish you good luck and God speed." Then he shouted, "Three cheers for Wren officer A001. Hip hip hurray".

They all climbed back into the lorry, and it moved off. I was left alone and was once again confused. I started walking, it was more like hobbling. I went in the opposite direction as that seemed the most logical thing to do. It must have been in about half an hour when I heard a car coming up behind me. I decided to ignore it. The driver stopped just in front of me and wound down his window and said in German, "Can I give you a lift young lady?"

I answered in German, "That would be very kind."

He pushed open the door and I could see that he was in uniform. German uniform!

I got in and we set off. He asked, "Are you trying to get to Hahn? I am based there."

I replied continuing all the time in German. "Yes, I am on a training exercise."

He seemed happy with that, and we travelled on in silence. We arrived in about twenty minutes at a check point. It was manned by a squad of four men in German uniforms. They asked for our papers. The driver produced his and told them that I was on an exercise. They were happy. I was taken to a cottage and met by two girls who welcomed me home in German asking me how I had got on. I told them the exercise had been absolutely terrifying. They commiserated. I was shown to a room with a bathroom next door. I was told supper would be ready in an hour. I had a lovely hot bath. There were clothes that were my size. I joined the two girls for supper. I spent a week with them with not a word of English being spoken.

Then when I came down to breakfast on the seventh morning, I was confronted by two French girls. I spent a whole week with them again without a word of English being spoken. Then I was picked up by a British driver called Ron and driven to Edinburgh Waveney Station to go on the overnight sleeper to London. I had a restful night and arrived in good order at Whitehall on the 1st of August 1940. As soon as I arrived in the same office, I was ushered in by the PA to see the man with the burnt face. He greeted me warmly, "Well done, I predicted that you would be good, but you have totally exceeded my expectations. I'm make no apology for treating you so cruelly, as hopefully it will help you to survive in the months to come."

I just smiled at him. I had nothing to add. He asked, "Have you kept up with the state of the war?"

I answered, "Yes, I saw German and French Newspapers and I have read this morning's 'Times' on the train. I can see that the RAF are being severely stretched".

He asked, "Your father was killed by a sniper. Would you kill German pilots?"

I did not need to think, "No. However as you are aware I witnessed unlawful killing of British Army Officers by the SS. I would have no compunction in killing any SS officer or in fact any SS soldiers."

Then I smiled, "I think I wanted to kill my instructors in Scotland, but I have got over that and put the course behind me." He laughed, "I'm glad of that as one of them was my nephew!"

I trusted this man. I knew he was not going to order me to do something which I found morally abhorrent. We discussed at length practicalities. We both agreed that I should work totally alone and have no contact with anyone. I would be contacted by messages in dead-drops. I would be supplied by both sea and air. I would have two missions, the first was to disrupt the operations of the SS which in reality meant killing their personnel. To do this I would have two further courses, one on sniping and another on explosives. I had received some unarmed combat and close armed combat training on my survival course. My second mission was to aid British airman who had been shot down over

France. I was to help them get to Spain. I was going to be based in the German controlled areas of France which stretched along the coast of France from Belgium to Spain. This office would only know about my whereabouts by intelligence gathered from the dead-drops and the successes that I achieved. When I reflected on this pivotal meeting, it brought goosebumps up on my arms.

The courses were so called in-house. This meant that I was not known by my instructors and these although ex-service men had not been trained in the standard army or navy centres. I was going to be mainly living in very rural areas, moving about a large amount, to confuse the enemy. This suited me. I was not cut out to be an agent in a city. I knew I was good with a rifle. I had found stalking deer had been wonderful experience when I was younger in Scotland. Everything about explosives was new. It was well outside anything that I had done before. However, I did find it worthwhile. I could see that placing bombs would be very disruptive and anticipating them would be very worrying for the enemy. Their disadvantage was that explosives were heavy.

At last, my burnt-faced man, I never had been told his name, signed me off to go active. The rest was rather up to me. I was dropped near the headwaters of The Marne River. It was symbolic to me as it was where my father had been killed at the end of 1918. It was a very rural area with large forests. These were ideal for concealment. There were canals and lakes and so I would have plenty of access to water. There was an important railway line running through which was going to be my target to sabotage. I was issued with little equipment. The sixty pounds I was going to be carrying was largely explosives.

I was going to be dropped in with no one to meet me. So, I was totally on my own. Everything I took was French to reduce the risk of discovery. I did have excellent forged papers, but I had no intention of using them. It was vitally important that I was not caught, not only because I would be tortured and then shot, but also because there would be reprisals taken by the Germans against the local populace. My main consolation was that I did not know anything and therefore could not betray anyone. As soon as the plane had returned to England, everyone on the side of the allies was in no danger from me. On the other hand, every German and every French collaborator was on the opposite side and was a target from me. I might only use my sniper's rifle on the SS but anyone of the enemy who got in my way or was a danger to me or an ally was fair gain. Great Britain and the Empire at that moment in time in the autumn of 1940 stood alone. My dead brother and indeed the father I had never known were rarely out of my idle thoughts. However, I had no time for idle thoughts. Survival took all my talents.

There were no goodbyes. I just threw myself out of the Lysander when the pilot gave me the thumbs up. He was high for his own protection. It was also a help to me to have plenty of altitude, as I had my own rip cord to pull and could track across the sky to land near to the silver river in the moonlight. The landing on the flood plain was relatively soft. I smiled when I thought of my legs which I held tightly together. I had no reason for them to be tied. I was a professional now. My kit including my rifle which I needed to put together at the earliest possibility was in my kit bag which I had let go on its rope as soon as my parachuted filled.

When I landed, I gathered everything together and set off into the safety of the forest. I took stock of my situation and put my rifle together, and then headed deeper into the trees. I walked for about an hour before I made camp and slept. Just in case the Germans were out looking for a parachutist I started walking again to put more distance from my landing place. At irregular places I hid caches of explosives and ammunition. I knew that the enemy might well use tracker dogs, so I constantly crossed streams going for considerable distances in the water. I remembered following beagles when I was a teenager. The hare would often elude them by running around in a large circle to confuse the tracks. I did the same. Once I was happy that I was not being followed, I set off for real on a new course.

I aimed at a tree in the distance on a knoll which had a commanding view of the terrain all around. When I got near to it, I started once again to circle going outwards at irregular places. It was dusk when I eventually climbed the tree and made myself a comfortable nest. My training had served me well. I slept soundly. I was grateful that I slept deeply, and I hardly moved. It was just getting light when I woke. I vowed that one of the criteria I would require of the man in my life, because I was sure that I would eventually find one, was that he lay still when he slept. I could not imagine sleeping with a guy who tossed and turned. It would be totally exhausting. I would get so irritable through lack of sleep.

When it was light enough, I slowly scanned the whole three hundred and sixty degrees surrounding my tree for German activity. I was very relieved that I saw no hostile movement. In fact, I saw no sign of humans whatsoever. I spent the whole day there constantly checking all around. Only then did I feel safe that my presence in France had not been recorded by, not only the Germans, but also not by the French who might well also be hostile.

Chapter 3

Meanwhile the London Blitz had started in earnest. The flat in which the 'Burnt Faced Man' lived was on St James' Square. It was obliterated after being hit by an incendiary bomb causing massive fire damage. His charred body was retrieved, and he was buried at his ancestral home near Dartmouth in Devon. My top-secret file together with some others which he had taken to work on at home was burnt beyond all recognition. From that moment on my total whereabouts was lost in time. My mother and my brother Hector knew that I was doing some work for the war office but nothing more.

Through a strange twist of fate, the PA to the 'Burnt Faced Man' was killed by an ambulance attending a 999 call. He was buried in the cemetery surrounding the large church in Croydon where he worshiped on Sundays with his sister who was the local librarian. He had never discussed his work with her, so she was unaware of my existence. The 'Burnt Faced Man's' department was taken over by the SOE. I was never taken on their books. I certainly had not been given an ordinary file let alone a top secret one.

I now was a non-person as far as the British Government were concerned. Of course, my mother blithely imagined that I would arrive home unannounced one day. Hector who was now on General Wavell's staff in Cairo never gave me a thought. I was in the thoughts of my instructors, but many more women and girls were being trained for clandestine operations and so my memory became blurred and slowly forgotten.

Reg in his sea view home in Dover did not forget me. He often thought of me particularly as he now travelled around the country checking naval establishments on their security arrangements.

He never had cause to go inland and so never again met up with my mother. She would remember him if she had been asked, but she wasn't asked and so he and his deceased wife who had been at school with her were never raised in conversation nor did they enter her thoughts.

I of course was unaware of all this. All I knew was that I never received any messages via any dead drops. Nor did I hear any messages in code through the BBC. This was not surprising as I had no radio and rarely went into bars or cafes. I became totally feral which I knew was much safer. The fact that I took as few risks as possible did not lessen my usefulness in disrupting German operations, mainly by killing them.

I was eased into the outlaw life in the autumn. I had time to adapt and more importantly lay down food stocks. Nuts and apples were plentiful. I stole farmers corn and potatoes. I caught rabbits in snares. I killed partridges with my catapult. I never had been a chubby round girl. Now I was rather like a greyhound, thin but muscular and able to cover long distances running and occasionally swimming although it became too cold as the shortest day arrived.

I used the explosives to good effect. I concentrated on blowing up track where it caused the most damage. I mainly used the train itself as the trigger. This meant that I was very unlikely to get caught as I was usually several miles away before the explosion occurred. I had ample opportunity to carry out anti-dog tactics. When I had used up all the explosives, I started derailing trains on bridges. I stole a large spanner so that I could undo the nuts holding the track. There was no way that I could lift the track. I had to use the train itself to cause its own derailment. It was very effective. It worried me slightly that my upper body muscles became rather over developed. I had been rather vain and had thought that men were attracted to my body. I was concerned that now they might not be. However, as I never met any men this fact was not very relevant. I did not meet any women either. I remembered reading a book about evolution. The author concluded that humanity was doomed as he claimed that women were more concerned about their appearance to other women than their appeal to men. This he hypothesised was a very bad evolutionary trait and would eventually lead to the demise of the species. My brain was fixated on the demise of German men, in particular German men in black uniforms, wearing shiny black boots.

I used the rifle to good effect. Initially I concentrated on single targets. However slowly my ammunition supply dwindled and then I started to use the rifle to carry out mass murder. I would kill the driver of lorries on dangerous roads. If those troops in the back were unlucky, the lorry with its dead driver would plunge off the road and kill them all. I am sure a psychiatrist if he had examined me would have been very concerned with my state of mind. I would have been sectioned immediately and then locked up in a secure establishment. However, we were at war. I was in total command of my actions. The end justified the means. I was too busy staying alive to brood. I kept on the move. Perhaps my father should have called me Diana, the huntress. However, he had chosen Athena well in advance of his sad demise. She was the goddess of war. She was all the while perfecting her art.

Greek gods and goddesses had their favourite animals. I remembered when I was a young teenager and had been told 'the facts of life', I was very wary of swans, not because they were supposed to be able to break your arm, but because I was concerned that I might be ravished by Zeus disguised as a swan and then become pregnant. My favourite animals were pigs. Their goddess was Demeter. She was also the goddess of fertility. I was not interested in fertility but more focused on the fact that pigs were omnivorous like humans. I was quite happy eating pig food which I stole from piggeries. I was careful I was never found out. I would watch and then when the farmer had left them for the night I would creep in and share their food. Also, I would

24

sleep with them. The weather was now much colder, and I got a much warmer night hidden under the straw with the pigs. They also could hear the arrival of the farmer, as their in-built clocks told them when feeding time was coming up. This woke me and I would immediately creep away before I was discovered.

I was glad when spring arrived. British people imagine the weather in France is Mediterranean. It certainly is in the south. Where I was in the north of France it certainly was not. It was much colder that southern England. It was good that I was a Scot so the temperature was in many ways similar. Occasionally I would venture into small towns like Langres. I would find a safe hiding place with an easy exit. I would wait for an SS officer to leave a bar, follow him back to his billet through the dark alleys. He would stop to urinate. I would quietly cut his throat from behind. I never went to the same town twice. I was never caught.

I had cached the rifle when I had run out of ammunition. I stole a luger from the first officer. I then had a ready supply of ammunition. However, it was not like sniping as I had to be very much closer to my target. It was much more opportunistic. I killed a Sturmfuher. He was carrying a machine pistol. This was more useful for close work when on two occasions I killed groups of four soldiers on patrol in lonely woods. I had to leave the area very quickly to avoid capture.

I was concerned about reprisals on the local populace. However, these did not start until later in the war. Because I moved about so much, I hoped the Germans would think that there was a cadre of British infiltrators not just one woman. As the war went on and the allies started bombing in earnest my second mission of rescuing airman became more important. This was rather ad hoc as I was not part of a team which passed the pilots on from one group to the next mainly aiming for Spain. I soon scouted out their routes. I would follow behind groups ready to warn them about German pursuit. I could easily overtake them and check the safety of the road ahead. Their discipline was good, and it seemed as if their security was tight. I was never sure whether they realised the goddess of war was interested in their progress. I was always relieved when they had crossed the high passes in the Pyrenees. I did not follow them further. Spain although fascist was meant to be neutral and of course Portugal was our oldest ally. I knew the route ended when they got on a boat to England in Lisbon.

It was in February 1943 when I was following a small group of one French guide and three airmen who were hiding in the forest to the west of Roquefort. They were safe as the forest in that area is very wild. I could get close to them but could not find out why they had stopped. I assumed that they were waiting for more airmen as the groups were normally bigger. Indeed, they were joined after seven days by another guide and two more airman. However, the first guide left them and returned north. Then the second guide led four men off south in the normal direction towards Grenade. I was unsure whether I had observed them correctly. I waited. I was sure that I had the right count, but it was very cold, and I began to think my tired brain had been mistaken. I plucked up courage in the night and crept near to their camp. I thought that I was taking an unnecessary risk. The camp had been tidied up as was their normal procedure. I was just about to leave when I heard whimpering almost like a dog.

It was a single man hidden under the leaves having a nightmare. Now I was not in danger from the Germans but from one of our own pilots. He had been left behind for some reason. I knew I was in terrible danger if he woke as he would assume I was the enemy. He was certainly armed with probably a gun and a knife. I hid in the leaves and waited. I got colder and colder. I was so tempted to leave him and make my way to a nearby large hollow tree where I could get properly wrapped up and wait for the dawn. He continued to whimper. I realised that he was not having a nightmare but was suffering from a fever. I moved nearer and smelt decay. He had gangrene. Then he lay still, and the whimpering stopped. I thought that he had died. I got close and could barely feel his breath on my cheek. He was alive but only just. He was really in a coma. The smell was coming from his left foot. I checked him and found a pistol under a sacking roll under his head. I also found a knife in a sheath on a leather belt around his waist. I took them both away and hid them under a branch.

It was macabre but all I could do was to get down beside him and cover us both with every piece of clothing we had, including my now very old parachute. I pulled bracken and leaves around us. I then slept expecting to find him dead when I woke.

I had dreams of Olympus. Zeus came. He did not ravish me as he was my father. He talked with his son Apollo who is my brother. Apollo sent his son Asclepius, the God of Healing to help me. He didn't help me but tried to ravish me. I woke with the man I had thought was going to die on top of me holding me down. He had plenty of strength. When I am surprised and frightened, my Scottish accent comes out. I was both. I screamed, "Bloody get off me, you, numpty! I saved your life."

He released me and in a Scottish accent said, "I never expected to meet a highland girl in France."

I replied, "Well you have. I am Lady Athena, brother of Hector, the Marquis Huntly. Who are you?"

He answered, with a smile, "Squadron Leader James Ferguson. How can I be of service to you Lady Athena. Shall I run your bath. You smell like a dead pig."

I laughed, "You are one to talk about bad smells. I must have a look at your left foot. I think you have got gangrene."

He replied, "That would be awfully kind. I caught my foot in a gin-trap beside a river, six days ago when I had been swimming. It was extremely painful last night. I feel no pain this morning. I think my whole foot must have died."

He was right. When I took off his left boot and sock, his foot was black. There was the most terrible reek. There was a copious about of malodorous pus. To my horror his foot and some of the bones of his ancle fell away leaving a raw stump. Asclepius had certainly come in the night. I was left with a one-legged man but at least he was going to live. If I could get him to safety, he might even with a prosthesis be able to fly again.

We were in little danger here deep in the forest, so I thought it was best to remain where we were. We were near to a stream. We had some food, and I could easily scavenge for more. James was very quiet. I guessed it was because he knew that he had lost his foot. He was very brave as it must have been very painful as I cleaned his leg. We risked making a small fire so that I could use hot water. My parachute was useful to make dressings and bandages.

It was cold but there were no clouds, so the sun did give us some warmth. His companions had made him some crutches which enabled him to hobble around. I was surprised that he was rather shy. Eventually I said, "Just pretend that I am a nurse, and you are in a field hospital."

He replied, "You aren't a nurse. Your Lady Athena."

I answered, "I wish I had not told you that. I am just a strange vengeful young woman who saw her brother gunned down by a three SS soldiers at Dunkirk."

Then he made me tell him the whole story. He crawled to me and put his arm around me. I started to weep silently, "I have not had anyone show me any affection for more than two years. I'm sorry I am being pathetic." He said nothing. He squeezed my shoulder. I asked, "Are you married?"

He replied, "No, I used to be rather a rake when I first became a pilot. Girls rather threw themselves at me. I changed when the war started. Life became rather serious when I lost so many of my friends. Many of them had left behind heart-broken girls. Now girls will certainly not want a one-legged man to hop down the aisle."

I said rather sadly, "From what I have understood from the French newspapers there are not many aisles left to walk down."

He shook his head. "It is not that bad. The Germans use a large amount of propaganda in the French press. There is a considerable amount of damage in London and the major southern cities like Plymouth and Bristol but 'The island race' is determined to fight on. Life in Scotland and in rural areas is not that different. The arrival of the Americans is really making a difference."

I realised that something was troubling him. I had broken down because he had been kind. However, I had a purpose, not only to kill Nazis, but also to repatriate airmen. He had doubts about his life, and it was not just because he had lost his foot.

I said, "I am sure you will be able to fly again. They will fit a prothesis. You will be able to walk unaided. My job is to get you back to the British Isles. Did you make them leave you because you were slowing them down?"

"Yes, I was in a lot of pain. I felt that I was not only slowing them down but also putting them all at risk of being captured by the Germans."

"I hope I won't let you down. I have been on the run for two years. I must be good at it, or I wouldn't still be alive. We will have to make a plan. The passes through the Pyrenees are treacherous. We will have to find a different way."

He smiled then. "You are so positive. I think, if I am honest, I am reluctant to return and continue to bomb civilians. I was not able to say that to my colleagues."

We both were silent. I got up and made us a cup of tea, from the boiling water that remained from washing his leg. I had stolen some tea some weeks earlier. It was light and I had carried it hoping I would be able to light a fire one day. Of course, we had no milk, but James had some sugar.

Chapter 4

The weather held and so in three days when James seemed much stronger, we set off north through the forest. My plan was to try to stowaway on a boat from Bordeaux. Although we had both agreed that James would not be able to climb over the Pyrenees, he made a reasonable speed on his crutches. He said he felt guilty getting me to carry everything, but I reassured him I was perfectly capable and happy. I was just doing the task that London required of me.

We never discussed it, but it became the norm that we cuddled together to keep warm at night. The spring was coming and although we did get rain, we made good progress. There was a large amount of wooded country all the way to Bordeaux. We decided to give the town a wide birth leaving it to our right and then get down to the mouth of the river Gironde where we hoped to somehow get on a boat.

On the way we chanced to pass to the west of an airfield. This gave me an idea. I asked James, "If we could steal a plane could you and I fly it away to England?"

He replied, "I am beginning to think you could accomplish anything that you set your mind to. I am sure that we could fly a plane together. I could instruct you or you could just work the rudders with your feet, and I could do the rest. The bottom of my left leg is too sore at present, but I am ever hopeful that the modern surgeons will be able to make it into a useful stump. I remember reading about the Napoleonic wars. There were officers walking on only one leg. I am trying to think in a positive way. I have been lucky. It is when you lose your leg above the knee when things are different. There is a great flier Group Captain Bader. He has lost the bottom of one leg below the knee and the other leg above the knee. He can fly and walk unaided. He can even play golf!"

I smiled, "I'm glad of all that information. Let's find a place where we can hide and observe the airfield."

The airfield had a perimeter fence. The Germans main defences lay to the north and west. They feared an attack from the river Gironde. They obviously thought that Bordeaux was too far south to be a target for a land attack. I scouted the west. There were defences against a sea assault, but we could get between those defences and the airfield. There was a big, wooded area crossed by tracts in the forest which we would have to avoid. I was concerned for James as he could not hide as quickly as me.

We found a good place to hide our camp deep in the forest. It would not be safe to light a fire so we would have to make do with cold food. I was careful, as always, to steal from houses well away from our camp and to take precautions about being followed by tracker dogs. To my delight I found a small pig farm. That would help us with food. I knew that the smell of pigs would lead dogs to the farm and not too our camp provided we went through a tributary of the Gironde which was wide and shallow.

Before we started spying on the airfield, I scouted out an escape route south in case we had to leave in a hurry. Then I made several spying trips to the perimeter fence. There was absolutely no possibility of James climbing over it. The fence went into the ground so we decided that we would have to tunnel under it. There were tracks both inside and outside of the fence which the Germans patrolled in vehicles, mainly motorbikes with sidecars.

Our tunnel was going to be a big operation. James was happy that it was worthwhile as he could tunnel as well as me as he had no problem crawling. We had plenty of wood for shoring up the tunnel. We were careful to procure it from deep in the forest but carrying it took time. I had no compunction in stealing tools from French farms well away from the airfield.

It took us all summer. I did much of the heavy work, but James was a careful patient man and so he made copious notes on the workings of the base. The planes were Heinkels (He 111s). James told me that they were torpedo bombers. They had two engines. He was totally confident that the two of us could fly one. What the two of us were not confident about was how we could overcome the crew of five. There were two pilots and three gunners. The fore-gunner acted also as a torpedo aimer.

We spent the whole of the summer and early autumn digging the tunnel. There was now no shyness bathing in small steams. We behaved really like mature siblings who had grown fond of each other. There was mutual respect. We never argued and we looked out for each other. During high summer it was even warm at night. We never however stopped lying close together. We often would wake in the night worrying about being attacked but we would quietly wake each other. And then relax when we realised that it was only a deer or a fox. We just smiled at each other in the morning when we woke. There was lust in his eyes but that never worried me. I never felt threatened. I was certain that he was fond of me. We both, I thought, were frightened to break the spell of our relationship.

When the tunnel was nearing completion towards the end of September, we started planning our heist. James did not know the exact lay out of the inside of a He 111. He told me in some detail what he thought it was like. There were normally nine aircraft parked up on a side apron. They took off in flights of three to patrol the Bay of Biscay for allied shipping. The number of sorties was dependent on the weather. There was no night flying. However, they often took off at first light and the final sortie might not get home until it was nearly dark.

Many nights we whispered together. It was not only the crew of five which we would have to contend with but also the ground staff. We decided that there was no chance that we could successfully get on board unless there was some sort of distraction. I was sure there was some sort of French resistance activity in the area, but we did not trust them. We were so careful with our security. It was the only reason that we were still alive. It was going to just be the two of us.

The plan was for us to emerge from our tunnel at about 2.00 am. The Germans did not light up the airfield for their own security. Darkness would aid us. We knew that the planes were fuelled up ready for immediate take off after the last sortie of the day. We planned to get on board one of them in the dark. At first light, James would fire up the engines while I guarded the entrance door on the bottom of the fuselage. I would shoot any Germans that tried to board, hoping the shots would not be heard with the starting of at least six engines. James would start to taxi using a stick to push on the left rudder which of course also controlled the direction of the tail wheel. I would secure the hatch and join him in the cockpit to help with the taxiing and the take-off when we were going fast enough to stop any Germans trying to get on board.

The plan was simple and so we both thought it might work. We had the element of surprise but little else. We just hoped that the ground staff would not fire at their own aircraft. That was our mistake. I had to shoot all five of the crew. Their bodies were lying on the tarmac. The ground staff were alerted, and we were fired upon as we came on to the main runway. Then we were shot at by an aircraft which had taxied behind us, together with a guy in a side car of a motor bike chasing us on the ground.

Neither of us were hit but there was considerable damage to the plane. I expected James to be a good pilot. He was no age, and he was a squadron leader. In fact, he was a real ace. He managed to take-off with a flat tyre with the wind which is totally the wrong direction for take-off. How he kept us in the air was a total miracle. He had told me at length about all the inside workings of the plane. I crawled like a ferret after a rabbit to the rear gun. I had had plenty of practice crawling. I manned the rear gun. The plane that was following us took some time to catch us up as they had turned and taken off into the wind. They had not expected the rear gun to be manned and I shot them down with my first burst of fire. Then I had to get back and manually winch up the left under cart. It was hard work as the mechanism had been hit. I eventually managed. My job was not yet done. I had to jettison the torpedo bombs as soon as I could so that we were lighter and could therefore fly higher if we needed to.

The dawn had broken, and we felt very exposed. I took station with the rear gun, but James managed to hide us in the cloud at six thousand feet as we set a course for England. He decided to take the most direct route over Angers and the French channel coast near Caen. There was a blanket of cloud between six and nine thousand feet which was a blessing. We hid in this all the way over France. It broke up over the coast and the Channel Islands. James climbed as high as he could. We could talk over the intercom. James said that he would normally have plugged into the oxygen, but we could not do this as the kit was lying with the dead crew on the tarmac, as were their parachutes.

The nearer we got to England the safer it became from the danger of attack by the Luftwaffe, as in the main the RAF had control of the skies over Great Britain. Our danger was that we were in a German plane marked with German Swastikas.

James said he did not want to worry me, but he was convinced that as soon as we crossed the coast, we would be on the RAF radar and would have been observed by the watchers on the coast. James naturally did not want us to be shot down. Also, he was aware that an He 111 would be very useful for the allies.

As soon as he had the coast insight he pushed down on the stick, and we hurtled down towards the ground. He levelled off just above the sea. A fishing boat flashed just under my eery. There was a dreadful screeching noise as the damaged under cart dropped. There was flak around us as we landed at Roborough RAF station. I should have been in the cockpit to help him with the foot brakes. I knew the reason why he had not asked me to come to the cockpit. He thought that I would be safer in rear of the plane. Somehow, he managed with his stick and his good leg. We stopped just before the far fence.

James shouted, "Get out Athena with your hands up." I did as I was told and was faced by a very angry old man, dressed in khaki waving a pistol about, shouting, "Lie down or I will shoot."

I was convinced that he would. I was not convinced that he would hit me, but as he just might, I lay on the ground. Not much of a welcome, but I was so thankful that we had made it, mainly thanks to James' brilliant flying.

The irate man shouted to his men. "Tie her up. She must be a spy. Be careful she may be armed."

My arms were roughly tied behind me and I was manhandled into the back of a car after they had relieved me of my knife and pistol. I was held face down with two men sitting on me. The car set off.

The irate man who I guessed was the commander of the local home guard, said, "Well done men. I was certain she was a spy as soon as I clapped eyes on her. The fact that she had a gun, and a knife confirms the fact."

Sadly, I could not defend my reputation as my face was pushed down on the seat. I prayed that they would be gentler with James as I knew just touching his raw stump caused him considerable pain. In fact, James had few problems. He just said that he was Squadron Leader James Ferguson who had been shot down in the raid on Cologne on the 5th of March 1943. This was soon verified. He was then taken to Plymouth General Hospital for surgery. I think I would have been slightly miffed as he was being looked after by a very pretty nurse. I did not know. I was taken to Plymouth police station and locked in the cells. I was denied the right to make a phone call, nor was a lawyer called. I think if the Commander of the Home Guard had had his way I would have been shot. Luckily the Police superintendent had more sense. He must have contacted someone higher up in the security services called Mr. Trafford, I was sure that was not his real name who decided that I was worth interrogating. I was therefore transferred under armed escort to a safe facility at Aldershot.

On the long journey I had time to reflect on my situation. I had been denied the opportunity of contacting my mother who I was certain would have got me released. I guessed that James was in no position to help me, not only, was he recovering from an anaesthetic, but also, he actually could not vouch for who I was. I had told him I was Lady Athena Huntley. I could equally have been a German agent who was using him to penetrate the British establishment. The fact that I had saved his life was not relevant.

I did not know the name of the 'burnt faced man'. I was certain that I could find his office. I did not know where I had been trained or where I had been flown from to get into France. I knew none of the names of my instructors. I did not actually know their faces. I really did not have a lot going for me. I decided the best thing to do was to tell the truth as far as I knew it. I was certain my mother would agree with that. I was tired, dirty and pretty depressed when I reached Aldershot. If I was really honest with myself, I was worried about James. I had grown very fond of him. Would he come through the surgery? Would he be worrying about me? Did I really want that? So many questions were chasing around in my brain.

Mr. Trafford was about fifty and unless he was a very good actor, he was ex-army. I was handcuffed to a chair bolted to the floor in a windowless room. He faced me across a table. He had a cup of tea. I was not offered one.

He asked in a rather smarmy way which instantly annoyed me, "My name is Mr. Trafford. Who are you, young lady?"

"I am Lady Athena Huntley, brother of Hector, the Marquis Huntly. I am a Wren officer; my service number is A001."

"Now young lady, we can do this the easy way and you can tell me the truth, or you can play games and I will make life very unpleasant for you."

"Can you telephone my brother Brigadier Huntly or my mother, Dowager Marquise Huntly. Her number is Aberdeen 843. Hector is colonel of the Highland Regiment. I do not know his telephone number."

"Very well, I gave you a chance." He drunk his tea. Picked up his mug, got up and left.

I just sat there hoping that mother had taken her telephone number to the Lodge House, otherwise he would ring a hospital, or that Hector was in Britain. Sadly, my mother had not taken her number and Hector was in Italy having led his men on to the beaches of Scilly against specific orders by the Allied High Command. Mr. Trafford did not tell me any of this when he returned with two Military Policemen. He said, "So you have decided to play games."

He turned to the men and said, "Leave her handcuffed but cut away all he clothes. You can cool her off by dousing her with buckets of cold water."

The men set about their orders with some pleasure. I just sat and shivered. They left. My only consolation was that it had not been obvious to them that I had urinated as a result of my soaking. I was exhausted and so I must have dropped asleep. They returned twice more, and half drowned me with cold water. When I woke again, it was pitched dark. I was shivering violently.

Mr. Trafford smelt of fried bacon when he woke me in the morning by ordering the men to soak me again. I wanted to protest but I knew that would be futile. I just sat and glowered at him.

He suggested, "OK, let us try again. You arrive in a damaged German plane carrying a German pistol and a hidden knife. Where had you come from?"

"Bordeaux. James Ferguson and I had stolen an He 111 from the Germans and they shot at us as we were taking off. Can you tell me if James is, OK?"

"I believe he has had surgery and is recovering. How long have you known him?"

"Since February, soon after he was injured by a gin trap in the forest near Roquefort."

Mr. Trafford nodded his head. I guessed that he had had someone interrogate James. He asked,

"What rank is James Ferguson?"

"A Squadron Leader."

"Do you know any details of his family?"

"No."

The interrogation continued. I was totally honest about everything which I had done from when I had left home in 1936 and travelled in Europe. Mr. Trafford then left me. I was moved to a better cell which had washing and toilet facilities. It had a bed and a high up window which let in the pale winter sun. I was given better clothes and for the first time in months I was clean and thought that I did not smell like a rotten pig. I was left to contemplate my fate for 48 hours. I imagined Mr. Trafford had been doing his homework. Maybe he had received reliable confirmation from my mother or brother. He might even have received information from 'The man with a burnt face'. I of course was unaware of his death. What he could not verify was what I had been doing in France before I had rescued James. No one could.

Then suddenly I was taken back into the interrogation room. Mr. Trafford would have made a good poker player. He gave nothing away. He was not angry nor was he friendly.

He said, "I have no time for any more stories." He gave no indication as to whether he believed me or not. He continued, "You have a choice young lady." He had never called me by my name. "You can be shot as a German spy, or you can work for the allies."

I did not hesitate, "I want to work for the allies."

He gave me a thin smile, "I thought that you would say that. In the summer the allies will be opening a second front to defeat the Nazis. We will be invading northern France across the Pas De Calais. The Germans are hurriedly constructing what they call the Atlantic Wall using forced labour. You will be dropped back in France with false papers and logistical support. You will liaise with the French Resistance to interrupt the work on the Atlantic Wall with any available means."

I replied, "Very well, I request that I am allowed to see James Ferguson in hospital and my mother in Scotland before I leave."

He replied, "That will not be possible. The drop has been fixed for tonight."

He got up with a threat, "Do a good job and perhaps you won't be hanged as a traitor when the Nazis are defeated."

He left. I now knew my fate. I reflected that he had not realised that he had offered me the chance to do just what I had fervently desired ever since I had seen my brother shot. I would have liked James and my mother to have known where I had gone. I trusted them both to have faith in me. I was not a traitor and I hoped I never would be.

I was taken back to my room and when it was dark, I was transported to an airfield under guard. I had to take Mr. Trafford at face value. I just knew he might be lying. I tried to see the situation through his eyes. I decided he was likely to be genuine and was an officer in the SOE. I did not believe his threat. However, it was not a pleasant thought to be resting in the back of my mind.

I was given my false papers by a Captain who said little. He also gave me the passwords for the resistance and the leaders code name. The maps I was given, seemed genuine from what I could remember. I was given a German pistol which could have been mine. I examined it carefully and checked that the mechanism worked. My knife also could have been mine. I was given French clothes and a rucksack with warm and wet weather, gear. I was relieved that my boots were good and fitted me. I had also been given a pair of smarter shoes. I was given a parachute and a good woolly hat.

I was taken out to a DC 3. There was a large amount of equipment which was mainly explosives, small arms, and ammunition. I was the only passenger. The jump master seemed friendly, just a little taciturn. He told me the drop zone was near Grenoble. He was probably like me, rather frightened as we had a long distance, flying over enemy territory before we reached our objective. The plan was to drop the equipment first and I would follow bringing my small rucksack on a rope below me. I had been given a chance to check my parachute as I was going to be pulling my own ripcord. I was told to sit in the jump seat just behind the pilot. The crew were obviously experienced. They did not want me to get in the way or to be a danger to them. I had a wee at the last minute before I strapped on my parachute and got on board. I was high on adrenaline I was going into the unknown, back to war. My thoughts were on James. I did so hope his surgery had gone well. I tried to analyse my feelings. Was I in love with him? Maybe. We had certainly spent a long time together in very dangerous situations. I was sure we each had the other's trust. There was no way I could know what our relationship would be like in a normal peacetime situation when I was cooking his food and washing his socks! At least I was only going to be washing one sock.

We started to take some flak as soon as we crossed the French coast. We were high and it was very inaccurate. I, like the pilots, and I imagined the rest of the crew, was given oxygen. Once we were clear of the coast. The flak mercifully stopped. I was glad that I had not been sick.

There was no way I could sleep. I just watched the pilots. They could talk on the intercom, but I could not. I knew we were approaching our drop zone as we suddenly started losing height. I unclipped my oxygen. I felt the cold when they must have opened the door. I could see the lit fires of the drop zone. One of the pilots touched my leg and nodded when I got up. I just gave him a small wave and made my way aft. They were just finishing the drop. I did not hesitate I was keen to get it over with. The jump master gave me a sign and I jumped.

I got into a stable position and tracked back in the direction we had come. Then I pulled the cord. My parachute deployed and I let my rucksack fall off my chest. It was bizarre. I suddenly, totally at random, was glad that I didn't have big breasts. With my legs clamped together and my knees partially flexed, I hit the ground and rolled as I had been taught. I had only started to pull in my parachute when I was aware that I was being watched by two men. I gave the password and greeted the man nearest to me by his code name of Maurice. He just pointed to his companion. That was not a problem I had just picked the wrong guy. I kissed them both on each cheek. I was a French girl again.

Maurice was a short swarthy man in his forties. His deputy was Claude. Everyone used these code names, so I did the same. I as Alicia on my false papers. I was from Lille I was a school mistress who taught German and English. Maurice and Claude seemed pleased with the supplies. They were quickly loaded on to small horse-drawn carts. I just waited until I was told what to do. Maurice told me to follow him. We left the others and headed east across this upper area which had been the drop zone and went into the forest. We moved rapidly I was glad I was fit. I carried my parachute and my rucksack. Maurice carried only his Sten gun. He had ammunition pouches on his belt. I had not expected to be trusted. However, I must have been as he took me to his farm. He had a young wife, Olivia but no children. She welcomed me and showed me to an attic room. Maurice burnt my parachute. I would have to find a blanket if I was going to sleep out. We had some rabbit stew and rough bread and then we went to bed, after I had been shown a trapdoor under the carpet where I was meant to hide in case of a German raid. It was going to be a tight squeeze with all my gear. I was woken at dawn. I was going to stay with them in the short term.

I was expected to work on the farm. I was pleased as I was to feed, water and clean out the pigs. I also had to feed the chicken and collect the eggs. At breakfast Maurice and Olivia discussed my persona. I did look a little like Olivia, so it was agreed that I was her younger cousin. Maurice seemed pleased that I had been trained with explosives. It was taken as a given that I could fire my pistol. They were not aware that I was a sniper nor that I could kill a man quietly from behind with my knife. They assumed that I was going to be part of the resistance in this area. I was going to train this group with the use of explosives. They had not been briefed any further. They readily accepted that I would move on north to train others. They were pleased that I thought the allied invasion was due to occur around Calais in the summer. They told me there were not a lot of Germans in this area, but there was further north particularly on the coast where the majority of the fortifications were being constructed using slave labour.

We discussed what I would do if the Germans arrived on the farm. The only things which would incriminate me was my knife, the pistol, and the ammunition. Maurice gave we a tin box and some oily rags from his workshop I buried the tin box in the woods about a hundred yards from the farm.

Maurice wisely did not start any sabotage operations until two weeks after the drop in case the plane had been spotted. That did not mean that we sat around in the evenings. I spent all my spare time after dark teaching small groups of resistance volunteers how to use the explosives. They were all local men and knew the area. They could easily decide which bridges and railway tunnels were going to be the targets without making special visits as those would only attract attention. By no means were all the locals trustworthy. Maurice knew of several collaborators. He worried that there could be many which he did not know. This level of distrust was new to me. It had been so much easier when I had been on my own. Granted I had to be my own sentry every night, but I found this clandestine activity much more stressful.

The first five operations were very successful. However, they drew the area to the attention of the Germans. There was a large SS presence in Grenoble. Thirty innocent inhabitants were shot as a reprisal in the main square. It was then that I told Maurice of my ability to use a sniper's rifle. He had wondered why a sniper's rifle had been included in the drop. He brought it back to the farm. He and I then took it high up in the forest well away from any prying eyes or ears and spent an afternoon making sure the sights were adjusted correctly.

Chapter 5

Then just Maurice, Claude and I planned a revenge attack. There was a restaurant called Le Coq on the square owned by a known collaborator, frequented by the German officers, particularly the SS. Claude who was well known in the bar was going to leave a small time-bomb in the bar. We wanted to use a big bomb, but that would be much harder to get in place. Claude would remain in the bar but in a place away from any blast to establish his alibi. I would be positioned high up on a roof opposite the restaurant with a line of sight to the door. Maurice would be guarding my exit out of the back of the building. My job was to shoot as many high-ranking officers as possible as they ran out of the restaurant. Maurice and I would make a hasty exit out of town on two bicycles which we would then use to return to the farm. We hoped that we would have time to hide the rifle well away from the farm.

It was a simple plan, and we had every reason that it would work. Initially it did. I managed to shoot three high ranking SS officers. We must have been betrayed by someone in the street. Maurice shouted to me that there were Germans behind us he got out and pedalled quickly away wearing a hood and so he was not recognised. I was trapped in the building by SS storm troopers. I used my rifle to good effect which kept them at bay, but my only escape route was up and across the roofs. I left the rifle and got out through a skylight and ran across the ridge. I was soon spotted and then they followed me on the ground as well on the roof. I emptied my pistol before they grabbed me. I was dragged downstairs and into a truck and taken to the Gestapo HQ. I was thrown into a dark windowless cell and left.

I had no water or food. I started to regret that I had not thrown myself off the roof. It was the following morning that they came for me. The SS officer was a sadistic bastard. I was stripped and tied to a chair. He was smoking and he burnt me with his cigarette until I screamed and then he would ask a question. They had found the rifle and they had linked it to me. The questions were all in French, so they had not guessed that I was British. They wanted to know who had planted the bomb. I stuck to my first statement that I did not know. They did not seem to know about Maurice. As far as I could guess they had not caught anyone else. It was strange as the officer switched his line of questioning. He claimed that I had been in the bar. He seemed certain that I had planted the bomb. He wanted to know how I knew about explosives.

He was not a good interrogator as he inflicted so much pain that I kept passing out. They revived me with buckets of cold water. I soon got so weak that I just whimpered. I no longer screamed when he burnt me. He gave up and I was thrown back in a cell.

The next thing I knew was when they dragged me out into the square. I was naked. They cut off my hair. They lined up ten women and children and shot them in front of me. I gave up. I told them that I was British. This they did not believe. They thought that I was from Paris. I was taken back to the cells and left to die. I didn't die.

They must have found something else about me. They did not let me die. They tried to get more information. I was beaten. They kept on about the planned invasion of northern France. When I gave them the details of the plan to invade across the 'Pas de Calais'. They had sucked me dry. I was so ashamed. I had betrayed my country. I had betrayed all those men who would cross into the waiting preparations by the Germans under Erwin Rommel, their most brilliant tactician. They hailed Hitler as a genius as he had predicted that the invasion would be across the straights of Dover.

My interrogator then ordered that I was to be kept alive as a witness to his expertise. I was allowed to recover. My hair grew to my relief. With better food my body filled out. The burn marks healed. I knew that I would always have the keloid scars. I tried to concentrate on the good things. At least I had not betrayed the French. I prayed that Maurice and Olivia remained free. I thought there was good chance that they had, or the Gestapo would have paraded them in front of me to show how clever the Germans had been.

My interrogator had been promoted. I saw him strutting around in his new uniform. His promotion resulted in him being transferred to a much larger Gestapo office in Lille. I was sent under escort to Lille. I was not sure why. Then I discovered. I was going to be made into his mistress. How he ever thought that I would do anything but hate him was beyond my comprehension. I plotted my revenge. I was determined to kill him and escape so that I could warn the allies that I had betrayed them. I would leave it up to Mr. Trafford to decide on my fate but at least I could die with a clear conscience.

The SS were to a man, a very arrogant bunch. I was going to use this arrogance against them. The interrogator was I suppose good looking. It was hard for me as I had never been good at acting. However, I had to try to pretend that he was god's gift to women. I had to be very careful and not make my act too blatant. I was helped by the other girls who were all local collaborators from Lille. Being from out of town gave me a little mystique. The SS officers seemed to have a lot of money. I soon found out that there were several extortion rackets.

It was not hard for me to discover that the town's people loathed us but most of them were too frightened to demonstrate this except for some of the very elderly who, having lost loved ones either in this war or the last, felt that they had nothing to lose. I was trying to plan an escape when events caught up with me one night. I was standing outside of a bar when there was a commotion in the alley way beside it. Two SS officers were trying to rape a young teenage girl. An old woman who might have been a relative was trying to stop them. I came up behind the two men. One had the holster of his pistol open. I guessed he was going to threaten the girl. I grabbed the pistol and hit him very hard on the back of his head. The other man turned to defend himself and was trying to get out his pistol. I kicked him in the groin and then hit him very hard on his head as he was doubled over.

I told the girl to run as I helped the old lady. Surprisingly no alarm had been raised. We managed to reach her house undiscovered.

She turned to me and said, "Aren't you one of the German whores?"

I replied, "Maybe but I hate them. Now I must try to escape."

She answered, "You must go quickly. Wear some of my shabby clothes."

That is what I did. I managed to get out of Lille undetected before roadblocks had been erected. There were no forests for me to hide in. The area to the north of Lille is all farmlands. I crossed the Yser river which I hoped would confuse any pursuit by dogs. It was not a wide river, but I was cold, and I resorted to my usual practice and joined some pigs to rest before the dawn came.

I was not discovered by the farmer or the Germans during the day and I made my way to Calais as soon as the night fell. I hid in a garden shed on the outskirts of Calais the next day and made my way on to the beach the next night.

Then I took on the biggest test of my life. I was going to swim the channel with the help of five glass fishing-net-floats and a helpful wind from the south. I did not know the strongest driver for this madness, whether it was the risk of capture and the subsequent torture and death, or whether it was my determination to warn the Allies that I had betrayed them.

I struck out off the beach bravely pushing the floats in front of me. There were no lights to welcome me towards England, just the pale luminescence of the white cliffs. I hoped by the dawn that I had got halfway. I doubted that I had got that far, but I might have. I was totally exhausted. I was very thirsty. I had forgotten to bring any water. I was saved by a rescue launch which was out looking for a downed airman. It was sad as they found him, but he had died from his wounds. I, who did not deserve it, had survived. The mug of hot tea was the best ever.

I adopted my real persona. First, I needed to confess my guilt and then I was prepared to accept the consequences. The launch crew were very focused on doing their job and so they were not worried about any papers or passport. The tea had revived me and so as soon as we docked, I made my way to Captain William's house. He gave me a wonderful welcome. He teased me, "So you have come back again to borrow more of Helen's clothes."

He was so kind, and I was so weary that I wept. He put his arm around me, and I told him how I had been broken by the Gestapo and that I had revealed to them the site of the landings in northern France in the area around Calais. He said very little, but just listened as I poured out my story. I felt cleansed when I had finished. He suggested I had a hot bath and then got some proper sleep. He said he would make some calls and then he would drive me up to London when I felt strong enough.

I felt considerably better in the morning after sixteen hours of deep sleep. I joined him for breakfast wearing some of Helen's clothes. He told me that he had contacted Mr. Trafford and he was keen to see me as soon as we got to London. I dreaded what he would do with me. Reg had also spoken to my mother. She had been relieved that I was safe and well. She had told him that

Hector was now back in the United Kingdom, but she did not know where.

I realised what a strange girl I was. I still thought of myself as a girl and yet I now was definitely a woman. I hated secrecy and yet I had tried my best to keep my secret hidden from the Gestapo. The country was full of secrets thanks to the war. I was reminded of what I had read of the First World War. Signs saying, Loose talk costs lives. I suppose I could defend my actions. Being interrogated by the Gestapo was hardly loose talk. My only consolation was that I had not betrayed my friends in the French Resistance.

Reg drove me to London. He dropped me at Whitehall saying that he was going to book in at the Army Navy Club in Pall Mall for the night. He said that he hoped he could take me out to dinner.

I was met at the entrance of the building by Mr. Trafford's PA. I did not know if that was a good thing or not. I had been correct. I had remembered the way to his office. I followed him through the labyrinth of offices protected with sandbags. I was in a complete funk. I trusted British justice. However, I was a traitor. Mr. Trafford had threatened me. I still could be hanged.

When I entered his office, he stood up and came around his desk to shake my hand. "Welcome home. I understand that you have suffered a large amount of unpleasantness from the Gestapo."

I blurted out, "I have been a traitor and will cause the deaths of thousand allied troops. I could not withstand the torture and told the Gestapo that the second front would be in Northern France at Calais."

He replied nodding his head, "I see. You had better sit down and tell me everything which happened after you jumped out of the aeroplane."

I slumped down and started my tale. He was a good listener. He just stopped me on occasions to clarify a point. I looked at him throughout the discourse. I was sure he knew a large amount of my report already. Of course, he had spoken to Reg. I went into much more detail with Mr. Trafford than with Reg.

When I stopped, he said, "Athena, you are a remarkable young lady. I have good news for you. We have dropped ten more agents to that area in France with large amounts of ordinance including radios. None have been compromised. The Gestapo are still unaware of Maurice's group who are continuing do useful work. I will have more work for you. However, you must take some leave. My PA will give you a rail pass for Aberdeen. I suggest you take the overnight train from Euston. Please report to this office on the 11th of June.

I managed to have an early dinner with Reg who then took me to Euston. In the car I asked him, "Mr. Trafford said nothing to me about my betrayal. It seemed as if he was not concerned. It was very odd." Reg was silent. Then he said very emphatically, "We are in very special times, Athena. The whole course of the war is on a knife edge. The allies have certainly taken the initiative, but I am very concerned on what is going to happen now. When you get to Scotland, I should make sure you regularly listen to the BBC."

My mother seemed pleased to see me. She was cross that she did not know where Hector was nor what he was doing but she was sure he was in England. The big house seemed as full of patients as it had done after Dunkirk. However now everything was much better organised. I could see that I was just getting in the way, so I was pleased when I got a call from Mr. Trafford's PA asking me to call on him the following morning, the 2nd of June. I managed to get a lift in an empty ambulance which having dropped off a patient was returning to London. It was not the most restful of nights but at least I was lying down.

I was ushered into Mr. Trafford's office as soon as I arrived. As usual he did not waste time with small talk, "I want you to go back to France. I know you should be allowed more leave after the trauma which you have suffered but time is the essence."

My heart sank. Was I brave enough to face the Gestapo again? Then I thought of Aeneas and my resolve returned. I also wanted to prove to Mr. Trafford that I was not the traitor I might have appeared to have been. However, I just somehow knew he trusted me or at least he was so desperate that he had to trust me.

I replied, "I will be terrified, but I am grateful to you for giving me another chance."

He gave me an enigmatic smile, "Just come home in one piece."

He wanted me to drop in France tonight in a DC3 with a full hold of guns and ammunition together with a sniper's rifle at the location where I had dropped before. Maurice would be there. He would arrange transport for me to Caen. I breathed a sigh of relief. At least I was not going to Lille.

I was heartened that the crew of the DC3 were the same guys. They had survived which was a miracle. My mind wandered and I thought about James. I wondered if he was flying again. I hoped he was still alive. I suddenly wanted to see him again. I was determined to survive this assignment and return so that I could find out about him.

The flak over Franc seemed to be more intense than last time. I welcomed our arrival over the drop zone. Once again, I was the last to leave after the munitions, with my rifle, unassembled, ammunition and few bits of equipment, including a side-arm and my knife. The night was cold for early June. Maurice and Claude gave me a warm greeting as did Olivia. She had food ready for me as I was going to leave as soon as I had eaten with a teenage boy called Jean.

He guided me to a rendezvous with a farmer with a van full of vegetables. I was hidden underneath them. Apparently, there were road German blocks all over the place. The French resistance had been much more active, and the Germans were determined to clamp down on the insurrection. First, we went west leaving Lyon to the north and then I was transferred to a lorry full of sand near Clermont just before dawn. The driver was very taciturn. He did advise me to get deep into the sand on the left-hand side of the lorry where there was a breathing tube hidden in tarpaulin. He said on occasions the Germans stabbed the sand with their bayonets. The thought of being stabbed made my skin crawl.

The sand was destined to be made into concrete to make gun emplacements on the German Atlantic wall. It was the most terrible journey, taking all day and most of the following night. I really don't know how I survived, but I did, and I was mercifully not detected at the numerous check points.

I was dropped in a forest south of Caen. I felt like little red riding hood as I was met by an old woman who could easily have been a wolf. She had sharp features and piercing eyes. She certainly knew the forest as after a couple of miles, on little more than animal tracks we arrived at her hut. I was totally exhausted she gave me some venison stew and let me sleep in her loft for the whole day.

When it was dark, she led me north through the forest to a convent. I was hustled into the back gate by an old nun without a word and shown to a nun's cell. There I was dressed as a nun and told that I was going with a group of them to sing in the choir in the Abbey of Saint-Etienne in Caen at noon. This Abbey had been built by William the Conquer before he invaded England. At the Abbey I was given a hessian bag to hide my rifle and ammunition, and some food, and I was given directions to the Rue Saint-Manview. There I was welcomed by an old lady and shown to an attic room with access to the roof tops. She was an interesting old lady named Madame Violette Beauregard. She had no love for the Germans. Her husband had been killed in WW1 and her son had been killed flying for the RAF in 1941. We spoke French but Violette told me that her English was quite

52

good if a little rusty. I asked her if she objected to me killing members of the German SS with my rifle. She laughed, "If I could, I would shoot them myself."

She very wisely burnt the nun's robes as she did not want the Germans to make reprisals on the abbey or the convent if I was caught. I was back in my fatigues before I ventured out to make a reconnaissance when it got dark. It was the night of the 5th of June. Only then when I could see the flashes of the guns of the allied capital ships firing to the north and the shells landing on the fortifications behind the beaches did I realise that I like the Germans had been deceived. The Allies were not invading Calais. They were landing in Normandy. Mr. Trafford had been very clever. I knew what my task was now. I had to kill as many Germans as possible to act as a distraction which would help the troops to get ashore.

Violette, she insisted that I called her by her Christian name, joined me for a breakfast of rolls, butter and jam before I left her to crawl unobserved along the roof tops. The road was well named as it certainly had a very good view. My first problem was of course that I had not sighted my rifle. My first target was a senior SS officer in the back of a stationary staff car. My gun was sighted high as my first shot hit the driver in front of him. I scampered along the roof before anyone could locate me. I then altered the sight. My first target had long gone, but soon a convoy of three tanks came slowly down the road. Their commanders were standing with their hatches open. I managed to hit all three before I hastily moved my position. I was lucky no one looked up and saw me. I moved on to another vantage point.

Then the Germans had much more than me to worry about. The USAF flying fortresses were very high overhead carrying out a daylight bombing raid. The bombs started landing about two streets away. My street was not hit but the earth seemed to shake. I was worried about Violette. I made my way back to her house across the roofs. That's what saved me as there a terrific explosion and the two houses that I had just been on were destroyed. If I had not been so worried about Violette, I think I would have been unable to move. I shambled through the sky light. She was in her kitchen getting provisions together. "Marvellous you have returned."

I replied, "I was worried about you."

She smiled, "I was worried about you also. We will go down to my hideaway until the Americans have gone. I knew one day the allies would bomb Caen, so I made some preparations."

We went down into her wine cellar. I could see that it had been reinforced with steel. There was a toilette and even a shower.

Violette said, "You must wait here with me. You will not be able to help anyone if you are a corpse. As soon as we are certain the raid is over you can go quickly back to the roof top as I'm sure there will be a large number of targets. I so wish I was younger. I would come with you as a spotter but sadly I would only hinder you. My role is to support you as I have done for all my brave family. I know by your accent that you are from Scotland. The Scots have always been good fighters and have often supported the French."

We sat then in silence. There was another explosion and the lights flickered, but they stayed on. Violette said, "Do not be afraid I have torches in case we lose the power."

She was a remarkable woman. She kissed me on both cheeks before I returned to the roof. There was chaos in the streets. I had no trouble selecting my targets. The SS were very distinctive in their black uniforms. It was noticeable that they were doing nothing to help the wounded neither the civilians nor their own German troops. They were there just to observe. It was beneath them to get their hands dirty. If they were on their own, I would take a single shot and then move my position. If there was a group of up to three, I would try to take all three and then move well away.

At nightfall which being June was late I returned to Violette. She had some hot soup for me and a glass of wine. I had a shower upstairs as I did not want to cause unnecessary condensation in the cellar.

Violette and I both agreed that it was very likely that the British would send in their bombers in the dark. We went down to the cellar before they arrived. Violette amused me when she said, "We will stay dressed, my dear. It would be so undignified to be dragged out into the street in our night attire if we got buried down here." I noticed that there were two beds. I teased her, "Were you expecting a good-looking Englishman?" She laughed, "No my dear, if one had arrived, I would have removed the second bed to make sure he looked after me properly! Englishmen have a reputation for being shy and not very good lovers!"

I laughed, "What about Scotsmen?"

She replied, "When I was a teenage girl, I used to fantasise about what Scotsmen had under their kilts. I had a friend who died of cancer. She used to say that us ladies have a duty to train our men to be good lovers. She said that a Scotsman would be a good man to start on as the lack of underclothes would make training easier."

I realised that I had a lot to learn from Violette. I told her about my dalliance with the stableboy and also about James. How we had spent so long together and yet we had never been lovers. Violette was very pragmatic, "I think he will be a good husband for you my dear. It is very important that your husband is your friend and is kind to you. You can always train him to be a fantastic lover because he will not have any preconceptions as to what you would like him to do for you when you make love."

I mused, "It will be hard to know where and when to start?"

She laughed, "You will just have to be very patient. You will need a time when you both are relaxed after a little wine and are in a nice warm place." She giggled, "You will have to slowly take off your knickers and watch for his kilt to rise before you turn and let him lift your shirt!"

We both laughed then. The RAF then arrived, and we could hear the bombs exploding. Surprisingly I was not afraid and slept. In the morning Violette said she had slept well. We had breakfast together before I took to the roof tops. I made her promise that if I had not returned and the USAF arrived that she would go to the cellar and not wait for me. I said that I would join her down there.

As it was the Americans must have had other targets. I imagined they were in Germany. I realised that they would not bomb Cherbourg as they would need that port. It would be vital for the allies to resupply the invasion force. I wondered how long it would take for them to take Caen. I had no way of knowing that they had planned to take the city on D Day. Mr. Trafford had thought that the allies would have taken Caen within 48 hours and so liberated me. Unbeknown to me he was extremely worried for my safety.

Caen was a key hub for the whole area as it was on the Orme River and had the Caen Canal running through it. The Germans filled the city with fifteen divisions. Obviously, I did not know the exact numbers, but I could see that there was a large amount of infantry as well as tanks. The Germans became much more careful and kept their tank hatches closed. I knew that Erwin Rommel was in charge of the whole German Atlantic Wall. I was sure that he would soon realise that he had been deceived and that Normandy was the main theatre of the allied attack. I longed for him to come in my sights.

Violette and I soon realised that Caen was going to be a battle ground. We were given a clue when the daylight bombing was renewed and was reinforced by shelling by the guns of the capital ships in the channel. This was totally indiscriminate. The whole city was laid to waste. Violette's house was hit. She and I were in the cellar. We were lucky as we were not trapped under ground and could get out. She made me dress as if I was her daughter. We rarely came out. There was a curfew, and we did not want to draw attention to ourselves. Not all the French population were against the Germans. Violette said that we could not trust anyone. Mercifully the bulk of the populace had left. I worried that Violette had only stayed because of me. She assured me that was not the case.

I had run out of ammunition for the rifle and all my sniping ceased. I hid the gun in a ruined building far enough away for it not to be linked to ours. I had my handgun. I went out one night and killed a SS officer and took his machine pistol together with two spare magazines. I had no intention of dying without a fight. I knew Violette was of the same mind. After a month we had run out of food. We still had water and there was wine in the cellar. We were very careful not to drink more that the odd glass.

Chapter 6

I will never forget the 21st of July. We woke to the sound of bagpipes. The Highland regiment had liberated what remained of the city. The bulk of the Germans had left but several thousand surrendered. Violette was very weak from starvation but the two of us came out on to the street. I was standing supporting her as a squadron of tanks trundled by followed by a jeep containing, to my delight, a brigadier. It was Hector. I formally introduced Violette. She said, "I'm glad you took your time young man. I have enjoyed your sister's company." From her bag she produced a bottle of red wine and four glasses. Hector's driver joined us for a toast.

I persuaded Violette to be evacuated back to England with me as survival for her in a destroyed city would have been very difficult. We were lucky as Hector's regiment had captured an airfield south of the city and so we were flown out with a plane load of wounded to Bristol. I managed to get through to Mr. Trafford. He said I should return home for some R and R and that he would contact me when he required my services. Violette recovered remarkably quickly when she started eating again, as did I. The train journey was tedious rather than hard and we eventually reached my home. Mother welcomed Violette and the two ladies of a similar age seemed to get on well.

It was Violette who encouraged me to get some news about James. I had to call in some favours, but I eventually tracked him down to Detling in Kent. It was good news. He was operational and had been promoted to Group Captain. That seemed pretty amazing to me for a man with only one foot. I did remember that he had flown us across the channel in a German plane with really no help from me, so actually I knew he was a great pilot. Trying to get him on the telephone seemed to be totally impossible. However, I did find out that he was now flying a new aircraft called a Typhon which was even faster than a spitfire. It was a ground support attacking aircraft and so was in constant demand across the channel where the British under Montgomery seemed to be bogged down pushing the Germans out of northern France. The Americans were making fantastic gains of territory in the middle of France under the charismatic General Patton.

I also managed to find out that James was billeted with a family in a farmhouse not far from Detling. With Violette's encouragement I set off to visit him. I did not let on to my mother as I was certain that she would not approve of me gadding about the length of the country to see a man even if he was a heroic Scotsman.

I took the overnight sleeper down to London. I called on Mr. Trafford for a mid-morning cup of very weak government tea. As always, he was very reticent about yielding any information. He did let on that he might have a job for me in helping the British advance. He told me to report back to him in a week's time on Monday the 12th of September.

I walked to Victoria Station and got a train to Maidstone East Station. The day was overcast and there was some rain. I thought it was unlikely that James would be flying. I decided to go straight to the farm where James was staying. I found an amiable taxi driver who was happy to take me on the three-mile journey. He dropped me at the farm gate. I slung my overnight bag over my shoulder and walked up the slight slope to the farmyard. There were young cattle in pens both sides beside the tarmac drive before I came to a granary on the left and a large fruit packaging shed on the right.

A man in his mid-forties came out of the shed. I guessed he was the farmer. He asked, "Are you wanting to buy some fruit? We have apples, pears, plums and even some greengages."

I smiled. I detected a slight Scottish accent. I answered, "I'm not actually. I'm looking for a Scott like you?"

He laughed, "I am detribalised, having been born in England, but we have a Scot staying with us. Are you looking for James Ferguson?"

I replied, "I am. Is he here? I guessed he wasn't flying today."

The farmer held out his hand, "I'm Roy Alston. James will be in soon. He is out with Prince bringing in the mornings pick."

I shook his very rough hard hand, "I'm Athena Huntley."

He suggested, "We will walk through the orchard and warn Jean that we have another for lunch. I will take your bag. James will bring the children when he comes in."

Roy registered my surprise as we bypassed the farmhouse, "My parents live there. We live a quarter of a mile away in a house which we had started building before the war was declared. We were lucky, we might never have built it if we had known that the war was going to be so serious."

I enjoyed walking in the orchard. The fruit trees had grass with sheep grazing beneath them. We were really in the 'Garden of England'. War had come here as well. There was an enormous crater. Roy said, "That was the first flying bomb to drop. We are on the direct flight path from Calais to London. Mercifully the British army have reached the launch ramps. However, there is a rumour that the Germans have made more in Holland."

To reach the house we passed an anti-aircraft gun. Roy gave the three-man crew a punnet of fruit. The sergeant said, "Thank you guv. The fruit means a lot to our families."

Roy asked, "Are we expecting more doddle bugs?"

The Sergeant replied, "We are. Your wife was out bringing us tea earlier. We tried to reassure her that if we hit one, the thing would explode well away from your house."

As we walked on, Roy whispered, "Jean is very sceptical."

I also whispered, "She must be worried for the children."

He laughed, "No, she says the gunners are hopeless and can't seemed to hit the doddle bugs!"

We arrived at the back of a large brick build modern house.

Roy shouted from the hall, "I hope you have enough food. I have brought Athena, a friend of James home for lunch."

Jean came out of the kitchen with a baby on her hip, "Welcome Athena. I'm sure we will have enough. We have plenty of eggs which are our own. I will make more Yorkshire puddings to make the meat go further."

She gave the baby to Roy and showed me to the downstairs lavatory. When I came out Roy handed the baby to me as he washed his hands. I felt very maternal as the baby who I gathered was called Fergus smiled up at me. He was soon sucking at a bottle as I cradled him in my arms, as I sat in a chair. Jean was busy in the kitchen. Roy had disappeared. I thought, 'Typical man!' There was soon a commotion as two children came rushing in, fighting to get to the basin to wash their hands. They were Jim aged 8 and Pat aged 4. They saw me, stopped fighting, and stared. Jim asked, "Who are you?"

I replied, "Athena. I'm a friend of James."

Jim asked, "Are you, his girlfriend?"

I hesitated and then said, "I wish."

I went bright red when James came around the corner. I knew he had heard. James held out his arms to me, "Athena, it is so wonderful to see you. I thought the Gestapo had got you," We did not get a chance to kiss as Pat asked, "Who are the Gestapo?"

Jim butted in, "That are really nasty Germans, silly."

Pat was not accepting that, "I'm not silly!"

So, no kiss. I had to be content with saying, "Well done with your promotion. I was pleased to hear that you are flying again."

He replied, "Thanks for that. Supporting the army is very different from bombing or dog fighting."

I said, "I gather you are flying a faster aircraft."

He smiled, "Yes the Typhoons are seriously quick."

There we were no affection. Just talking about the war. The children made a welcome break with their chatter. I did notice that Jean seemed very fond of James. I was not sure if it was in a brotherly way. The weather improved rapidly in the afternoon and James had to go to Detling. Jean kindly asked if I would like to stay for the night. I said that I would be delighted, but I didn't want to put her to any bother. The house had six bedrooms. I had rather hoped that James and I would have to share but that was not on the agenda. I thought back on what Violetta had advised me. Perhaps it was for the best. A family home was not an ideal place for a night of passion to find out if James and I were compatible. We had been fine cuddling together to keep warm in the forests in France. Sleeping in a warm comfortable bed was a totally different scenario.

It was dark before James returned. We had had an early high tea. The children were in bed and asleep. Jean made James some supper, so the adults all sat around the dining room table and talked. The news on the BBC was full of the rapid American advance. James had flown only one sortie. He said that his Group had seemed to have been very successful.

I was pleased that James put his head around my door and wished me goodnight. Roy had gone out after James had eaten as he was an Air Raid Protection (ARP) warden. It was about 4.00 am when the doddle bugs started coming over. Roy was still out on ARP duty, but Jean got all of us huddled under the Anderson shelter in the living room. Pat and little Fergus still slept but Jim was wide awake. He clutched his mother moaning, "Here comes another one Mummy." I thought what a marvellous father James would make when he said, "I'm going outside to watch them go over and see if the gunners can hit them. Do you want to come with me, Jim?"

This was just what Jim needed. He was a brave lad as he was only eight. The two of them left us in their pyjamas. I stayed with Jean. Sleep was impossible as the anti-aircraft gun behind the house started firing. The flying bombs made a distinctive noise. Jean explained to me that while you could hear their single rocket like engine there was no danger as they would fly over. It was when they went quiet that you were in trouble as it meant that they were gliding down and would explode on impact. The one which had made the big crater behind the house did just that. The family had been lucky, as it could have so easily hit the house. As it was, it had blown in the back door which was partly glass. Pat had been standing near and had been covered in shards of glass, yet she had not received a single cut. Jean had been upstairs nursing Fergus who was only a month old. Roy had been running back from the farm. It naturally had made a shocking impression on Jean and Jim.

I was glad when James and Jim came in under the shelter which was little more than a reenforced steel box. I suppose it would protect the family from falling masonry but obviously not from a direct hit. Roy came in at 8.00 am and we all got up properly and had breakfast. The raid was over. Roy confirmed that no flying bombs had landed anywhere near us. James told us that there were squadrons of night fighters stationed nearer to London who were tasked to nudge the flying bombs off course so that they would explode harmlessly in the marshes in Essex. Roy told me that he had marshland in north Kent just south of the Thames. They had made those marshes look like an airfield. The ruse had not worked as only a single bomb had landed harmlessly. I reflected at least Mr. Trafford's ruse had deceived the Germans into thinking that the invasion of France was coming across from Dover. I also reflected that he had had no compunction in sending me to France. He must have realised that eventually I would have been caught by the Germans.

I was helping Jean by feeding Fergus who seemed to have a voracious appetite. We were in the kitchen. Roy, James and the two older children had gone out on the farm. Jean was washing up, she said, "James was so kind to Jim last night. I was at my wits end as those blasted bombs are terrifying Jim. How long have you known James?"

I replied, "As you know we have not seen each other for over a year, but we spent time together in France. His leg had turned gangrenous, and he was not able to cross the Pyrenes into Spain. I looked after him and we stole a German aircraft, and he flew it back to England."

Jean was very protective, "Were you alone with him?"

I answered honestly, "Yes for several months."

I could tell by the look on her face that was not what she really wanted to hear. It was obvious that she had feelings for James which she felt guilty about. Roy was a good guy and a good father but had not been paying her any attention. She was a very attractive woman. I certainly did not blame her. Then she returned to her real concern, which was her son, Jim. She was worried that he was of an age when the horror of war was affecting him. I wondered if I could help.

I tentatively asked, "My mother is good with little boys. I grew up with my two brothers. I knew from quite an early age that they meant more to her than I did. I really only came closer to my mother when my brother Aeneas was killed in the aftermath of Dunkirk. My other Brother is fighting now in France. She lives in Aberdeenshire. There is a Prep School near her. Would it be better for Jim to go to school up there, where he would be safer and perhaps more importantly would not be subjected to the nightly fear of air raids."

She continued washing the dishes as she digested my idea. Fergus had filled his tummy and was dropping off to sleep. I was glad he was a good feeder as he gave a big belch but did not vomit down my front. I said, "Why don't you put him in his cot. I will finish the dishes."

When she came down, she hugged me, "I missed judged you, Athena. I thought at first you were an upper-class good time girl, looking for a husband. You are much more than that, you are a deep thinker. I can't think of what you have been through in this war. I am very fond of James. However, you would make him a good wife and be a good mother for his children. I just pray we will all survive. These dam bombs make me feel we are in the front line here. James is risking his life everyday flying these sorties. I suspect you will go over to France again."

I replied, "I expect I will. All I can say is that having flown with James I know he is an ace pilot. So, if anyone will survive, he will."

Jean asked, "It must have been terrifying sitting next to him while he was flying with only one leg."

I smiled, "I did not have a lot of time to be afraid. I was in the rear turret shooting at a German plane which was pursuing us."

Her eyes were wide, "You were firing a gun?"

I smiled, "It is not something I am very proud of, but I am a crack shot. I also happen to hate Nazis which certainly helps."

Jean might have missed judged me. I certainly had underestimated her. The following morning, I kissed everyone including James, goodbye before a taxi took me and Jim off to the station for the biggest adventure of his life. I was surprised. There were no tears. He had clamped his teeth together and shook his father by the hand, kissed his mother and ruffled his sister's hair much to her annoyance.

I surprised myself. I was quite good at entertaining little boys. We were in a carriage full of wounded soldiers who thought we were mother and son. The men were happy to answer Jim's questions about their injuries, the guns they fired and the tanks they had destroyed. Victoria was busy. There was a scrum on the underground. It was a first for Jim. The train up to Edinburgh from Euston was full of sailors. The fact that they thought I was travelling with my son made no difference. They still tried to chat me up. I rather felt, 'What the hell', and enjoyed their banter. Jim when to sleep with his head in my lap when we reached the borders. My head was resting on a soldier's jersey on his shoulder when I woke at Edinburgh Waveney.

It was way after Jim's bedtime, but I guessed he would be hungry as we only had eaten snacks during the day. We went into a small restaurant, and both had plates of shepherd's pie and peas. Jim like his baby brother was a good eater. We both have clean plates and so we had apple pie and custard to follow. We asked the waitress about a small hotel. She advised against trying as she said we were rather late. We ended up sharing a room in the Caledonian. We also had to share a bed as they only had double rooms vacant. I sleep well as Jim was not a wriggler.

We had a good fry-up for breakfast before going back to the station and took a train to Aberdeen. It was going to be a long tedious journey but at least we were on the final leg. We were in an empty carriage so that I read to Jim. He had brought with him a copy of short stories by Saki. I found them amusing and so I read with some good intonation.

We managed to get a taxi to my home. Mother gave us a warm welcome. I reflected how my relationship with her had changed since before the war. Jim seemed pleased with the large room which had been found for him. He immediately set about putting out a track with Hector's Hornby double 0 train set. Mother was on the phone to the wife of the headmaster of St Michaels, who was an old friend of hers. The timing was ideal as the new Michaelmas term started the following day. Mother went on her own to get Jim a uniform. He would be wearing a kilt. Jim was very proud of his attire. I sent a Telegram to Roy and Jean to say we had arrived safely and perhaps equally important that Jim seemed very happy.

Chapter 7

I got to settle him in at school before I left for the return journey back to London to report to Mr. Trafford. My ability as a sniper was required for a new offensive in Holland to speed up the British advance towards Germany. It was going to be an airborne assault to capture the bridges across the Rhine at a place called Arnhem. Once again, I was going to be dropped behind enemy lines. I felt like an old cat. I wondered if I was running out of my nine lives. I hoped that the luck of the Goddess of war had not deserted me. I studied the maps carefully. I remembered also that I was the Goddess of wisdom. The whole operation relied on surprise and a very rapid advance by tanks to support the parachutists. I was very sceptical as the British advance unlike the Americans had not been very rapid up until now. I was concerned that the British High command were perhaps not as forward thinking as their American counterparts. When I voiced my worries to Mr. Trafford, he gave me his normal enigmatic smile and said, "That's why I'm sending you my dear." I did not find this reassuring.

Initially the element of surprise caused widespread confusion within the German high command, with several HQs being unnecessarily evacuated. We took our day one objectives which included Ede and some of the Rhine Bridges. I moved stealthily between vantage points taking out black-uniformed senior SS officers, after quickly zeroing in my rifle. I was wearing my khaki fatigues over French civilian clothes. There were French refugees among the cheering Dutch civilians.

I carried ammunition weighing sixty pounds. I was content to keep firing to reduce my load. All the time I was making for the Hartenstein Hotel. The sky above me was free from enemy aircraft but I always had an eye out for any typhoons. I knew James and his whole Group would be in the thick of it. I gathered that the Typhoons had been sent in first to knock out the enemy anti-aircraft installations so that the American daylight bombers could flatten the area.

Creeping down the side of a road I came across an empty, except for the driver, parked German troop carrier. I guessed the occupants had set up an ambush for the advancing British troops. Even with my skill of stealth learnt in the forests of France there was no way that I could get up on to the vehicle without being seen or heard by the driver even with the engine going. I was only ten feet away. I drew my side-arm and risked a shot. I hit the driver killing him instantly but although I had not seen them the whole section of German troops were nearby. Several Germans returned to vehicle. I was then in a fire fight and soon my pistol was out of ammunition. I would have been killed but for the arrival of a section of the airborne division. When the fighting stopped, they could not believe that I was a single woman working alone. They insisted that I came with them after they had commandeered the German troop carrier. The officer called Chris Higgins gave me some rounds to load my pistol. His men only had 303 rounds for their Len-Enfield rifles. I was in desperate need of specialist sniper rounds for my De Lisle Carbine.

Eventually having draped the troop carrier in a Union Jack so that we weren't shot at by our own troops we reached the Hartstein Hotel. I asked Lieutenant Higgins to go into the HQ as I stayed with his section and hid around the back. I knew that Mr. Trafford did not want my presence widely known. Chris Higgins did not hang about and soon returned with the ammunition. I was grateful to him as now I could proceed to my real target which was the town of Arnhem on the German side of the Rhine which was being held by the 1st British Airborne Division.

Once again, I was the huntress as I had to move through enemy lines. This was made doubly hazardous as the bridges had been taken by the British and were now being held against German counter attacks. I had only to go 13 miles to Eindhoven. As soon as I reached within a mile, I was being caught in the crossfire. I chickened out and went up stream and managed to swim across when darkness fell.

I was chilled to the bone so to try to get warm I went on through the night. I had 40 miles to get to Nijmegen It was difficult and I only managed 12 miles. I was exhausted and I had to lie up in German held territory. I did sleep as I was so tired. I woke in light rain. I got moving again. I was not sure about the rain. It would at least stop James flying so it was safer for him. It made my travelling more unpleasant. It did have another positive attribute; it kept the Dutch indoors. The majority seemed delighted that they were being liberated, but I still found it difficult to totally trust them.

I killed a German sentry the following night and reached the British lines guarding the bridge at Nijmegen early the following morning. Naturally they were very suspicious of me and although they believed that I was British they still thought that I might be a German spy. I was manhandled and brought to their commanding officer. He was not pleased to be disturbed over his breakfast. My case was not helped by my rifle or the Dutch clothes they found under my fatigues when they stripped me.

However, my naked body was appreciated enough for them not to shoot me immediately. A Captain Richards who was their intelligence officer, was tasked to interrogate me. He was not gentle. He asked me all about the German positions that I had passed through. I could see that actually he knew all the answers which did endorse that I was telling the truth. With the daylight he could see the keloids on my breasts from the cigarette burns given to me by the Gestapo.

He said, "I will give you a chance young lady." He turned to his sergeant, "Jarvis you and Smith will bring her kit and keep her covered. We will take her across the bridge and see how well she performs against the Germans."

It would have been comical if I had not been so frightened. They took me naked across the bridge into the village to a front-line position. It was an electric relay station which they were using as a lookout point. The two occupants had rather unpleasant grins on their faces when Captain Richards and I arrived. There were two holes where the two electric cables stretched out to the next station. Captain Richards handed me my rifle. He asked, "Is the next station occupied?"

The Lance Corporal replied, "Yes Sir, there are two Krauts up there."

Captain Richards turned to me, "OK Athena. There are two Trojans. Kill them."

All I could think of was at least he had remembered my name and he knew his classical history. Then I remember my first survival training. I now, was not lying in nettles, just facing two armed Germans three hundred yards away.

I hoped Captain Richards appreciate the movement of my chest as I took a half breath. I squeezed the trigger. I saw the German's head explode before I worked the bolt. I had to wait for over two minutes before I saw the second German's head appear. I killed him. Captain Richards had not finished with me. He made me walk alone unarmed to the next station. I climbed up to find the two corpses. I came down and waved. Only then did Captain Richards and his two men join me.

He said, "Give her back her clothes. I have to hand it to you, Athena, you are a pretty cool customer. If you survive this war, come, and find me. I live with my parents in the Gate House for Leeds Castle in Kent owned by the Bailey family."

He watched me intently as I dressed. His parting remark was, "You have nine miles to reach the bridge at Arnhem. I will alert them that you are coming."

I replied, "Thank you." I held out my hand and said, "See you at Leeds Castle." He had a firm grip. He smiled. He was a real bastard. He certainly was careful. I thought he was more likely to survive than me. I set off. I moved away from the power lines and followed a ditch going roughly in the same direction. Although I was keen to press on and get to Arnhem. I travelled very carefully as there seemed to be Germans everywhere. On two occasions I had to kill lookouts. I was glad that Captain Richards had given me back my knife. The killings had to be silent.

I reached the British lines at 4.00 am. I had to swim the Rhine. It was a massive effort as I had to swim with my rifle and ammunition. Once again, I was arrested by the British sentries. However, Captain Richards had kept his word and I was taken to the HQ. Mr. Trafford must have also sent some advanced communication as the Brigadier was expecting me. I was given a place to lie down after they had given me a cup of tea and some biscuits and a tin of bully beef which was most welcome.

It was noon before I was taken to a vantage point overlooking the German lines. I could see through my scope that they were preparing an offensive. They had three tanks. I started disrupting their preparations by picking off the officers. I had to change my position several times as they also had marksmen. My training and experience kept me alive as did a Typhoon squadron which took out the three tanks. The Germans retreated and the British position held.

Nighttime came and I returned to the HQ. I had become a bit of a celebrity which I knew was not what Mr. Trafford would have wanted. However, it was rather inevitable. The news from the advancing British armour was not good. They were going very slowly and were not meeting their objectives. I went to sleep on my blanket as soon as I had had some food. I wanted to be up before the dawn. I had already selected a good vantage point to start my day. I was going to need a steady hand because my targets would be at least six hundred yards away. Some snipers like to have a spotter with them, but I liked to be on my own and do my own spotting. It has the disadvantage that the enemy can creep up on you when you are concentrating on the view through your scope.

I had a machine gun nest in my sights. There were three men. I manged to get two of them, but I was too slow to get the third. I decided on prudence and moved my position in case the third German had spotted me. From my next hide out I could see a road over seven hundred yards away. It was empty. I waited and then I was rewarded. A line of tanks came over the crest. They all had their turrets up as they were so far away from the British positions. There were five. I would need to be quick. I aimed at the commander of the tank in the rear, I had to give my shot a lead as they were moving. I took the shot, ejected the cartridge, moved my aim forward and took the second shot. The tanks kept coming, my shots would become easier but equally the likelihood of being spotted became higher. I took my third shot. I knew I should move but the tanks kept coming. My fourth shot provoked a barrage of machine gun fire. The wall I had been leaning on disintegrated as I scuttled backwards into the stairwell. The fire was so heavy the whole tower stared to crumble. The only thing that saved me was the slope behind the tower. I ran and was covered with shards of masonry. I had warned the troops where I was so that at least I was not killed by friendly fire. I felt guilty as these troops would be now a prime target. When I reached them, they could see what was happening. They had a wireless and so they radioed in for air support.

The Typhoon must have been in the area as it was over us within ten minutes. It managed to disable all five tanks with its cannon. It made me realise how vital it was to coordinate ground and air support. I reflected that the success of this whole operation really depended on our pilots of which James was one, being able to fly. If the weather closed in the whole of operation which was called Market Garden would result in heavy casualties.

This is just what happened in the ensuing days. The heavy armour did not reach us in time. The Germans surrounded us. We were supplied by airdrops but slowly the permitter around Arnhem got smaller until there was not a large enough area to support a safe drop. We were on our own. The idea to out flank the German Siegfried line had failed. It was hailed as the most valiant action in the war, and I was proud to be part of it. In reality its failure delayed the British advance and the end of the war in Europe by several months. Naturally we did not know this at the time. Thousands of troops were captured or killed.

I only escaped by discarding my rifle and all my kit and swimming across the Rhine. I was lucky to survive as it was very cold. I managed to keep ahead of the German advance. With the help of the Goddess of Wisdom, I was not killed by the British. Then that same goddess took me into war again.

In a thick wood I managed to evade two British sentries in the middle of the night. Then I came to a squadron of three tanks very well camouflaged. They had not lit a fire and there was no noise. It was the smell of oil which alerted me to their presence. The crews were sleeping under the tanks. I crept under with them. One man must have rolled into me and felt my wet vest which was my only article of clothing. He whispered in a very posh voice, "You're wet David. Is it bloody raining again."

I whispered back, "No it isn't, but I had to swim the Rhine." He must have been dreaming as he murmured, "That was silly, darling." He then wrapped me in his arms. I did not argue with him but enjoyed the warmth of his clothed body, particularly as he had drawn a warm blanket over us both. I was mentally and physically totally exhausted and so I soon slept.

Our wakening before dawn was quite comical. My new best friend whose name was actually Captain Marcus Oliver, was obviously devoted to his wife and pushed me roughly away from him and accused me of being a Dutch whore. I, in no uncertain terms, assured him that I was neither a whore nor Dutch but was a Scot called Athena Huntley. David, who was the gunner, lent me a very smelly shirt to hide my modesty. He did not care who I was or what nationality but offered me a drink of water and a very welcome but rather stale hunk of baguette. The other two, Bob, the driver and Ken the gun loader seemed fascinated by my nudity and were obviously not impressed that David had lent me a shirt. We all urinated and were soon under way after Marcus had instructed me that I had no choice but to come with them as I was a danger to them and might betray them to the Germans. Why he thought I would not have done that already if I was a collaborator was a mystery to me.

Marcus oversaw the squadron, and the other tanks followed us in line. I could not see anything as my face was pushed into Marcus' leg as the tank had very little room inside. In fact, there was only room for me as the top half of Marcus was outside of the turret. Heavens knows what would happen if we came under fire. I just prayed that the German's did not have a sniper like me in this theatre of the war. They didn't but when reached the edge of the wood we came under fire from German positions on the far side of a big field. Prudently we reversed back into the trees having called up air support. I was very grateful to the typhoons. I certainly would remember to thank James when I next saw him. They totally obliterated the German positions, and we crossed the open field and into another wood. I did not actually see any of this but Bob who was driving kept the rest of us in the tank up to speed of our progress.

The typhoon attack had brought in another three British tanks and several troop carriers. We now had infantry support as well as some field artillery as the troop carriers each towed a field gun. I was sad as that was the end of our advance. We had reached the river Maas and had been ordered to dig in and make a defensive position in case of a German counterattack. We were not very far south of Nijmegen. All those men who had lost their lives had died in vain as the town and bridge of Nijmegen were back in German hands.

I stayed with these troops for five days as they dug in. There was no counterattack, probably because the Germans did not fancy crossing the river Maas. Also, the weather stayed open so on the whole the RAF controlled the sky. I borrowed more clothes, and the guys shared their food with me. I had discarded my sniper's rifle and there was no spare 303s so I was not helping the allied cause except the sight of my legs seemed to cheer up Bob and Ken.

Marcus had to attend a brigade commanders meeting. He returned with our orders which were to keep preparing our position as the high command was certain there was going to be a German counterattack if and when the weather closed in. We were now in October and so misty autumn weather was the norm in this area near the Rhine and Waal rivers. He also brought back information of a fielded hospital which had been established in Tiel.

I decided to leave the front line and return to Britain and find out what orders Mr. Trafford had for me. I walked back to Tiel and spent a night there before getting a lift back in a medical convoy heading back to Blighty. I managed to steal a nurses' uniform as my attire was far from appropriate. Now I could help with the wounded. I wondered where James was. I was certain his group would have been moved forward across the channel to cut down the lag-time when their support was required.

I stayed with the convoy of wounded and reached Calais where hospital ships were ferrying wounded over to Dover. When I arrived in Dover after I had helped them all to get on to trains, I walked to where Reg lived. I was lucky as he was home having recently returned from London. For his sake my timing could not have been better. He had just heard that Helen had been killed by Hitler's latest weapon, the V2 rocket. These were being launched from mobile launchers in eastern Holland. Reg was distraught, although he seemed relieved to see me, alive. It was almost like coming home to the father which I had never had who had just lost his daughter. Initially he was inconsolable. I was gentle with him and soon the so called stiff, British, upper lip came to the fore.

I distracted him and learnt of news of my mother who was very well and continued to enjoy Violette's company. Hector was still in Belgium fighting Rommel who was rallying the panzers for their final defence of the Fatherland. The war was far from over. Reg begged me not to risk going up to London. I managed eventually to get through Mr. Trafford's PA. He said there was a flap on, but he promised that Mr. Trafford would ring me. He told me they expected my return and that he would arrange that a new sniper's rifle together with ammunition, would be got to me in Dover.

Reg was appalled that they were sending me back to the front. He was not thinking straight in his grief, as he begged me to take him with me as a spotter. This was totally out of the question. I did not want a spotter anyway, but I had to let him down gently.

Then I had my own grief to suffer. I rang Jean at the farm to find out news of James. I knew immediately that something dreadful had happened. I thought it was Roy or the children. It was James. He had been shot down on the front near to where I had been and had not managed to get out of his plane which had according to his fellow pilots had exploded in flames. I came off the phone and hugged Reg.

My war had become very personal. I found my grief very difficult to rationalise. I regretted that James and I had never become lovers. The romantic side of me wanted James to have at least gone to his grave knowing that he had a girl who wanted to marry him and bare his children. On reflection whatever was the point of that. I now had another drive to go back to the front. All and every German was going to pay. The Goddess of war had made me into her instrument. Wisdom was not top of my agenda, but I did have the sense to wait for my De Lisle Carbine to arrive.

I will never know if I would have left Reg to his grief and gone up to Scotland and wallowed in mine, if Mr. Trafford had not stressed the importance of my presence back in Holland. Nor would I ever have known if I had had the strength of purpose to survive the hardship in the cold which I was to experience in, what was later called 'The Battle of the Bulge'. The horrors which I had suffered at the expense of the Gestapo paled into insignificance when I was lying in the snow in January 1945 trying to get a shot at Erwin Rommel.

Rommel was a marvellous figure head for the Germans. Montgomery would never have admitted it but I'm sure he was terrified of Rommel's ability. Also, there was little doubt in my mind that the panzers as tanks were just slightly superior to anything that the British possessed. However, as my mother would say, "It is not only the equipment, my dear but the men who are using it that count." I had my doubts. I suspected that the reason why the British and American advance across France was successful was because of airpower. The mighty Luftwaffe was a spent force. If Hitler had spent the German energy in building planes rather than flying bombs and rockets the outcome of the war would have been very different.

The problems experienced by the allies in 'The Battle of the Bulge' was the weather. It was appalling and it grounded the allied airpower and so they were unable to assist the army. The bombers could still bomb the German factories night and day, but the typhoons and the spitfires could not see to support the tanks and infantry. They were stuck in the snow and so was I.

I took dreadful risks getting my targets. The only thing that kept me going was determination to decapitate the German army by killing its commanders. I had read about the British use of the rifle in the Napoleonic war. The rolling barrage of the British musket had eventually defeated Napoleon's Grand Arme'e, but it was the riflemen who had decimated its sergeants and junior officers and thus destroyed the will of the troops. I hoped that I was destroying the will of the German army and the commanders of the panzers in particular.

I never even got near to Rommel, but no German was safe from my rifle. I worked totally on my own mainly in the forest. I was always freezing cold. It was a miracle that I could squeeze the trigger. My hate and anger kept me alive until suddenly one morning on the 3rd of February 1945 the thaw arrived, and the sun burst through. The RAF was back in business. The German tanks were destroyed in their hundreds and the allies started to advance.

Chapter 8

My task was done but my war was not yet finished. At the army HQ I met up with Hector. He was putting together an elite rapid force to move forward and destroy the V2 rocket sites in Holland. The Germans had hidden them well, but the British knew roughly the forest where they stored the rockets before launching, by tracking them back using vectors.

The Prime Minister had taken the destruction of these V2 rockets as a personal mission. He thought, as it happened wrongly, that Londoners were on the point of collapse because of the terror of this new weapon. In fact, the V1 flying bombs were much more terrifying because you could hear them coming. The V2 rockets arrived without warning and mainly destroyed empty property.

I managed to get hold of more ammunition for my rifle, together with new dry khaki clothing. Hot food and a hot bath did revive me somewhat, but I was still a wreck. I was dammed if I was going to have Hector reporting back to mother that I had let him and the family down. I took my place in the back of a jeep with Jock, Hector's radio operator. I had met Andrew before, Hector's driver. He introduced us, "Jock, I want you to be very careful with that lassie. She is the Chief's younger sister. She is not here to be decorative but to kill Nazis and protect the three of us."

Suddenly my grief hit me, and tears wet my cheeks. Jock noticed and whispered, "The weather is good. Any problems I will call in aircover."

I sniffed, "That's my problem. My man flew typhoons. He was killed a month ago. It just hit me."

Jock asked, "Was he a Scot?"

I replied, "Aye, He was one of the best. I feel better just telling you."

Jock smiled, "That's grand. I didn't want anything to blur your vision. The word back home in the glen is that you are a crack shot with that fancy rifle of yours. My father says it's in your blood. He was your father's stalker."

I realised who he was. I had not recognised him because of the camouflage on his face. He reached up and rubbed some more boot black on my face. I smiled. He laughed, "That's better. Eight years ago, when you were a girl, I never would have thought that I would have been rubbing your pretty face."

I then appreciated what a close-knit group the clan was. I was proud to be fighting with them. I felt guilty, as I looked around and saw the rest of the group in the jeeps. They all knew me and yet I did not know them, although I guessed that Hector knew them all. They were all his picked men, but of course they were volunteers. I was proud then. I took strength from their comradeship. I checked my rifle yet again.

Hector arrived. He jumped into the jeep raised his arm and we were off. The other jeeps did not have radios but had mounted machine guns manned by the two men on the back. Our convoy of jeeps moved at high speed through the populous area of southern Holland to reach the British front line on The Mass River north of the Dutch town of Venlo. We were going to rest up in a wood near the village of Lottum. We then hoped to cross the river having forced a very small bridge in the middle of the night to coincide with a massive raid by the RAF on the industrial area of western Essen.

Naturally the Germans had fortified the bridge. However, it was not strong enough to allow tanks to cross and so the planners had hoped that we would be able to get our small jeeps across. I was certain that the Germans would have placed explosives under the bridge. I guessed they had not destroyed it because of

Hitler's specific orders that certain bridges would be left so that the Germans could counterattack.

It was a dark night and so it was useless for me to take up a sniper position. My courage was still on the line and so I was in the back of the third jeep. The front two would lead with their heavy machine guns. First two men had to creep forward and blow up the wire barricade. The timing was critical. It was immaculate. The barricade was blown just before the jeeps rushed across with machine guns firing. I was terrified but we got across in the third jeep unscathed as did four more jeeps. They then killed all the German defenders.

There was a danger that our attack would be bombed by the RAF. We were lucky and our route was not compromised. We managed to reach Xanten and took the jeeps as close to the Rhine as we could before abandoning them. We then had to carry our kit. I was lucky my rifle was light. It was much harder work for the men who had to carry Bren guns and for Jock who was carrying the radio.

We reached the Rhine. The best swimmer in the brigade then swam across drawing a light line. This was no mean feat as the river was wide. The place had been picked as here the current was not so strong. I was in position with my rifle at the ready, but our luck still held, and our presence had not been discovered by the enemy. The light line was then used to draw across a stronger line. I was the first to cross with my light rifle on my back. Hector and the rest were close behind me. The line was loosened so that it would not be visible when daylight came. There was no river boat traffic on the Rhine because the Americans had reached it further upriver. Then our trek began, first through the marshes before we reached some wooded ground. It was vital that we reached deeper into the forest before dawn.

We made it. I imagined the guys were as exhausted as I was. I did not envy the men who had to go straight on to picket duty. The rest of us hunkered down in our wet clothes in the bracken.

I did not care that Hector, Jock and Andrew all cuddled up close to me. It was a very uncomfortable few hours before we were off again. I hoped the Germans had no tracker dogs in the area. We travelled north and soon we crossed the unmarked border into Holland. We then stayed hidden in the forest for the day.

We had two more nighttime marches before reaching the objective which was the rocket launching area in Northern Holland. We had bypassed Arnhem which we had left to our west. It was very frightening being behind German lines. Hector had insisted that I was in a British battle dress and like all the men was wearing a green regimental kilt. He, unlike myself, still had faith that the Germans were holding to the Geneva Convention and therefore that we would not be shot as spies.

On the second night we witnessed the launching of ten V2 rockets which we knew were destined for London via the stratosphere. They were impossible for the allies to destroy once they were airborne. It was vital that we destroyed the whole of their launching apparatus.

We lay hidden up for our final day. It was a miracle that we had not been discovered. Each man had been carrying some explosive. This was no way near enough to destroy the four sheds which we had seen in the woods. The plan was for us to make a large enough explosion to cause a fire so that the RAF could be really accurate with a specially timed bombing run, so that we could get out of the area and not be hit.

I knew from all my contacts in the military that Hector was renowned for his very careful planning and for looking after his men. It said a large amount for his own courage that he was leading this operation personally. I observed how there was a strict line of command. If Hector was killed, then his second in command would immediately take over and so on down the chain. I never enquired but I assumed I was the tail-end-Charlie. However, I was heartened that all the men seemed to respect me. I hoped that this was not just because I was Hector's younger sister but at least some of my exploits, although classified as top secret, had been recognised.

As soon as it was dark, we all started crawling forward out of the wood on our bellies towards the two trip wires which had been located by a two-man patrol. These were not cut but had to be carefully stepped over. I felt very exposed standing up. When I reached the perimeter fence a hole had been cut. It was easily large enough to let my slim body through. Once through we formed up in our four groups to plant explosives on the four sheds. As we got near, we must have been heard by the guard dogs as they started barking. This had been anticipated and we all broke into a run.

Now we were each a separate unit. The timers on the explosives had been adjusted to allow for the different distances which had to be covered. Still, although the dogs were barking the Germans had not opened fire, presumably because they could not see any targets and they had not been ordered to do so. I realised that lights had not come on because of the German fear of discovery from the air. I could not hear the bombers yet.

At last, the explosives were planted, and we were moving northwest. Then ahead of us the night sky was lit up by a mass of search lights and the German anti-aircraft guns opened up on the British bombers who must have reached the coast.

In a strange way it was exhilarating having shed our heavy loads of explosive and to be running towards freedom. Then the Germans started firing. Although there was some return of fire, on the whole the men, including me, kept going as quickly as we could, not only to escape but also, we knew the bombs would be falling as soon as the explosions started in the sheds.

There was a slight delay at the perimeter fence as more holes were cut and then we continued at the double with no concerns about the trip wires as they were no longer relevant. The Germans had mounted a counterattack and there were vehicles coming towards us on the permitter road. This was my moment.

I knelt beside the road and started firing carefully aimed shots at the positions where I estimated the drivers sat. I knew that my controlled shooting was much more effective than the spray of fire from a Tommy Gun. I was on to my second magazine when the back marker of the fourth group shouted to me to follow him.

There was chaos in a mass collision of vehicles on the road. I manged to catch up with the rear man who I knew was called Anthony. I knew this was all part of Hector's plan. Our escape had been on time as I could hear the bombers above us. Then explosions started behind us. I just hoped that would stop the chance of any German pursuit.

The planners had had access to local intelligence from the Dutch resistance. The V2 Rocket sheds were guarded by experienced SS troops, but the rest of the area was patrolled by recent conscripts, mainly young Hitler youth. We now could move quicker in the theory that the Germans ahead of us would not be so disciplined or well organised.

The RAF had pulled out all the stops as not only did a second wave of bombers arrive, but also that was followed by a third wave. It allowed us to regroup for a ten-minute break in the forest just to the east of the large village of Putten. We now had three miles to cross the railway, a large road and reach the River Eemmeer. This was wide open farmland. The dark helped us to stay out of sight, but I could see the raised wall of the Eemmeer ahead of us. We were aiming for its narrowest point, but we still had a fifty-yard swim. We then had more farmland before we reached the marshes which we had to negotiate before we reached the Oostvaardersdijk behind which was the North Sea.

The navy had not let us down. We rushed down to the waiting boats as dawn was breaking. Then disaster struck as a German column came towards us at speed from the East. We were at our most vulnerable as we were wading out and boarding the boats. I still had my rifle, and I took careful aim at the cab of the leading truck. I had a lucky shot. I dropped the rifle as the truck turned sharply out of control and rolled over. Then I was swimming for my life in the waves. Hector was pulling me on board when he was hit by a stray bullet in the neck. His blood poured over me. He died without a word. We had accomplished our mission. Thousands of lives had been saved in London, but I had lost my second brother. I had not got time to grieve as there were eight other men badly wounded who I helped to nurse before they swung the boats onto a destroyer.

The whole operation had cost twelve other lives. It was labelled as a total success after the aerial photographs taken after the raid were analysed. Us survivors which included Jock and Andrew travelled up to Scotland having been taken to Harwich before getting on the train. It was a very sad journey as we had to travel with our casualties and the injured. I was dreading meeting my mother. I knew she would have been told of Hector's death.

She was amazing and organised the funeral without a tear. I was a wreck and was of no use whatsoever. Reg had come up from Dover. He did his best to support me. In some way because I did nothing to hide my grief, I recovered some sense of normality within a few days. I stayed in the Lodge House. My mother was so stoical which I found very worrying. She would leave Violette and go out on long walks with her favourite Labrador. Several times I asked if she wanted company, but she declined with a nod of her head. I spent most of my time up at the main house pushing the wounded about in wheelchairs. The one thing which kept me going was the news of the war. The Russians were advancing rapidly. Stalin was determined that they would take Berlin before the Americans. Unbeknown to everyone Roosevelt, Stalin and Churchill had made an agreement. The British and the Americans stopped their advance on the Elbe.

There was some celebrating on the 8th of May when the Germans surrendered but it was muted in the Lodge House. My mother and Violette supported each other. I was pleased when my mother asked Violette to stay with us indefinitely. She had no reason to return to France and so she accepted. I was in a state of limbo. I had come to an acceptance of my grief for my brothers and although I did not discuss it with anyone else my grief for James.

I travelled down to London and was officially released by Mr. Trafford. I bought a small Austin and travelled down to the farm in Kent. Roy, Jean, and the children seemed pleased to see me. Even little Fergus appeared to recognise me. Jim was home from school up in Scotland. He was fascinated by the war and had totally recovered from his fear of flying bombs. I suppose because Roy was an ARP warden, he was particularly focused on defending the country from a German invasion. Apparently, they had a drill for all the little boys in the school if the German Panzers had invaded. Each boy was allocated a certain point on the roads surrounding the school. If the siren was sounded, then each boy took four dinner plates and ran to his appointed place. He would then place the plates in an up turned position across the road. This was meant to delay the German advance as the tank commander on reaching the plates would have to stop to make sure that the plates were not mines. I could not help myself from thinking about this scenario and laughing. It was only then that I could really come to grips with the futility of war. Five years of my life had been lost in hate. I now felt it was time for laughter and love. I had a marvellous time on the farm playing with the older children and pushing Fergus in an old pram. He had a harness strapped to him and he loved it when I ran, and he bounced about. He screamed with delight. The older two loved to ride on the hay carts. Fergus loved it when I ran pushing the pram behind.

This peace after the tragedies of the war in Europe was dispelled the following morning when I bought a paper at a petrol station at Bearsted on the way to go and see Reg in Dover. I sat in a layby and read an in-depth article on the difficulties being faced by the Americans and the Australians in the war in the Pacific against the Japanese. Obviously ever since Pearl Harbour I had been aware of the problems in the war in the Pacific, but my mind had been so focused on the Nazis that I had paid very little attention to the Japanese.

I had been aware in the war in Europe that the Germans had fought much harder when they had been defending their own country. It appeared, or so I read, that now that the allies were closing in on Japan that they were defending their own territory ferociously, even to the extent of young men flying airplanes directly into allied warships to try to destroy them. These were called kamikaze pilots.

I reflected on my own behaviour, had I wanted revenge for the death of my brother Aeneas so much that I would sacrifice my own life to kill the enemy. I felt I could truthfully answer that question with a 'No'. I had always tried not to die. I had never given up my life even when I was being tortured by the Gestapo. I had never given up my life when my body was being frozen to death when I was lying in the snow in the battle of 'The Bulge'. I pondered on what the conflict was like in Pacific. It seemed as it was in no way finished. Many more lives were due to be lost on both sides. Was not a peace possible. Did the allies have to demand an absolute surrender by the Germans. I thought they did when they unearthed the horrors of the death camps for the Jews and other so-called undesirables. I had read other articles about the horrors of the Japanese POW camps. I did not doubt the stories of the Japanese brutality. I had suffered first hand on the brutality of the Gestapo.

I drew out of the layby and wondered if it was a sensible thing for me to go and stay with Reg. Would I just make him sad. Would I stir up all the old grief in my life. Would it not be better to turn around the car and return to my home. There I could perhaps answer these difficult questions and make some plan for the rest of my life. At this moment in time, I had only myself to consider. It would be totally different if I had a man to worry about, particularly if the man was wounded physically or mentally. If I had children there would be no choice, I knew I would love them passionately and would plan my life around their care until they were older enough to no longer need me. I was thankful that my relationship with my mother had changed for the better. If it hadn't, I might well have made erroneous decisions in planning my future life.

I saw a sign to Leeds Castle. I remembered Captain Richards. I blushed as I remembered standing naked in front of him. I did not even know his Christian name, but I did remember his firm handshake and that he had told me where he lived and had led me to believe I would be welcome to visit his family home. On a whim I took the road to Leeds Castle. The red-bricked gate house was obvious as I drew through the impressive gate. I parked my little car on the gravel in front of the Lodge. I went to the front door. I could not see a bell, so I used the imposing brass knocker.

There was a deep barking from within. A female voice stopped the barking, and the door was opened by a kindly looking woman with twinkling eyes. She asked, "How can I help you?" The yellow Labrador did not look hostile and cocked its head in an endearing gesture. I replied as I reached out to let the dog lick my hand, "I am looking for Captain Richards?"

She answered, "That is my son, and this is his dog, Megan. Why are you looking for him?"

I replied, "I met him at Arnhem. He gave me this address and suggested that I came if I was ever this way, so I have come to look him up."

Mrs. Richards stood back saying, "Do come in. Megan seems to like you. She is normally wary of strangers. Come through to the kitchen. I was just going to make coffee. Would you like a cup?"

I answered, "Yes that would be lovely."

Mrs. Richards obviously did not know what to make of me but was reluctant unlike her son to interrogate me. She made coffee in silence and we both sat down at the kitchen table. She had made a third cup and on queue Mr. Richards came in the back door. He looked questioningly at his wife. She said, "This young lady met Rodney at Arnhem. I would like to introduce her, but she has yet to give me her name."

I said, "I am Athena Huntley." I held out my hand and he shook it saying, "My son told me about you. Your bravery disturbed him. He was awarded a VC. He was involved in some very fierce fighting. I think he doubted his sanity, when he came across you. Mrs. Richards looked worried, "You never said anything to me Jack."

Looking very carefully at me, Jack said, "He was very embarrassed by the way he treated you, Athena, and yet you are very real, and you can't have thought that he had done you any harm or you would not be here."

Mrs. Richards was still confused and concerned, "Jack, why did you or Rodney not say anything to me."

Jack turned to me, "Can I explain to Lily?"

I shrugged, "Of course. It was a war situation, but I would not like you to be distressed Mrs. Richards."

Jack sat down, "From what I understand. Rodney as an intelligence officer had to interrogate you. Initially he thought you were on the side of the Germans. He had you stripped." Lilly gasped and put her hand to her mouth. Jack continued, "He recognised the scars on your breasts as cigarette burn marks from some time ago. He suspected that you had been tortured by the Gestapo. He thought it was possible that you were working for them. He took you naked to the front line to test you. He watched you as you killed two Germans with your sniper's rifle. He made you walk into danger in front of the British lines. He was very impressed with your bravery. He said he thought that you should have received a VC. He heard multiple stories of your bravery, but your presence was denied by the authorities and your bravery was never acknowledged. It was just as if you had never existed. He was intrigued by your name as like me he had a classical education. You must admit it is unusual."

So, I had to tell them my story. Jack said, "I am so sorry for the loss of your brothers, and the man you were fond of and indeed your father. You have suffered a lot, Athena. I salute you."

Megan then barked, Lily said, "That will be the post." She followed Megan to the door, quietening her on the way. Lily returned and her face had become ashen. She returned holding a telegram which she handed to Jack, "You open it Jack, I can't face it."

Jack tore open the telegram and read it out, "I'm sorry to inform you that your son Rodney is missing in action and believed to be dead." Without thinking I blurted out, "He can't be. The war is over." Jack had his arm around Lily, "It might be in Europe but sadly it is still continuing in the Pacific where we believe Rodney to still be fighting with the Australians and the Americans. He knows the Pacific well having worked and holidayed over there."

I realised immediately how narrow my outlook had been. I put my arm around Lily, "I'm so sorry. You must not give up hope. I have got some good contacts in London. I will try and find out some more details. If you can put me on a train, I will leave immediately."

Jack said, "I will take you to Maidstone East station it is much the quicker way."

Lily stood up, "It is best that you leave your car here. We will look after it. Then when you return, just ring us and we will pick you up. I am so grateful. It is going to be dreadful just sitting here waiting for news." As it was Lily came with Jack so that she could be with him and then neither would be alone. They told me more about Rodney. As soon as he left school he went travelling.

He travelled first to Australia and then into the Pacific area. He worked on small boats carrying mail and supplies around the islands in the Pacific. When he took some leave, he would go walking on any island which he saw which he thought looked interesting. He was a career soldier and had been at Dunkirk and before I met him had landed on D Day. His parents quite rightly were immensely proud of him. He had been highly decorated. Naturally his parents had not wanted him to keep fighting, but they understood his love of the Pacific islands and the people who lived there. He had been transferred, at his request, into the American army as his knowledge of the islands was so valuable.

Chapter 9

My first port of call when I reached London was to go to Whitehall and seek out Mr. Trafford. He greeted me warmly after his initial surprise, "I remember Captain Richards in your report. Naturally I cross referenced it with his report, not because I didn't believe you, but it was my job. I will give you in confidence a contact in the American Embassy. We are working very closely with them to bring the Nazi war criminals to justice. It is very tedious work, but it is vital that we do it well and bring the criminals to account. Also, I believe very strongly that we need to uphold international law. We must not cut any corners, or we will be behaving in a similar way to the Nazis.

I had to agree with him. I was very relieved that now that hostilities were at an end, there were not people like me acting like war time snipers. They would really be assassins. I hoped that I was better than that. At least now I had a worthwhile compassionate goal which was to find Captain Richards or if I could not find him to find out what had happened to him and if possible, repatriate his body so his parents could grieve. I knew it was going to be a tall order.

I stayed the night at Army and Navy Club in Pall Mall. My father had been a member. Mother had kept up his membership which was free, as she was a widow of a member killed in action. She had made her three children, members. I liked the place as it was very central. Although its address was 1 Pall Mall it really was off St James's Square. Members were allowed to go into the beautiful quiet gardens which were fenced off in the middle of the square. I liked to sit in the gardens and recharge away from the hectic life of London. A London which they now were trying very hard to repair after the German bombing.

In the morning I walked to Grosvenor Square to meet Mr. Trafford's contact in the American Embassy. I was wearing my uniform. I was given the run-around by various junior officers. I realised that I had made a mistake. I left and went shopping. In war torn London this was far from easy, but I knew the form and called in a few favours. I returned to the embassy a very different woman. I was no longer a young girl, but my body was still fit and athletic. It did go in and come out in the right places. I now was a very elegant smart young woman.

I had borrowed an engagement ring from the family jeweller, Bentley & Skinner in Bond Street. I was honest with the manager. He was sad when I told him the reason for my mission, but we both could see the humour. He teased me saying he expected me to bring in a real fiancé soon. I replied, "I'm getting more cantankerous every minute, like my mother. No man would have me!"

He replied, "I have a grandson who has been recently demobbed. We supply everything a woman can want at Bentley & Skinner!"

I laughed, "I prefer older men, Mr. Skinner. What are you doing for lunch?"

I left him laughing, "Good luck."

The young staffers at the embassy obviously worked on shifts. I was not recognised as the same individual who had been such a pain earlier in the day. I was shown into the outer office of Colonel. Brad. Stevens. His PA, I saw was Captain Al. O'Malley. He had a wide smile. He was of Irish extraction, and I guessed he could charm birds out of the trees. He took all my details and said he would do some research. He asked where I was staying in London. He promised to contact me as soon as he had any information.

I realised that I had got as far as I could that day and so I retired to the gardens in the middle of Saint James's Square. The sun was shining. I sat on a bench and hitched my skirt up to get a tan on my legs. Silk stocking were unobtainable in London unless you slept with a GI. My mother would have been appalled by my behaviour, and yet she would understand that I had no reason not to walk naked to kill two Germans on the command of Captain Rodney Richards. His image had faded but it had been refreshed by the photos that Lily had shown me. To help me with my quest she had given me one of Rodney in uniform on his last leave.

He had never been demobbed but had been transferred into the American army. I realised that was not a simple process. He must have had some important contacts. From what Jack and Lily had told me, he also had considerable knowledge of various islands in the Pacific. I knew the Americans were struggling to capture these from the Japanese who had had a long time to fortify them.

The sun went in, and I repaired to the club and rang Jack to give him an update. I really did not have much tell him except to say that the PA of an American Colonel was carrying out an investigation on the details which I had supplied. I asked Jack if he could give me any more information of Rodney's movements in the Pacific before the start of the war when he joined the British army. Lily came to the phone. She had postcards which he had written on his travels. She read out the names of the islands and I jotted them down on a piece of paper. I told her I would do my best to get some more information in the morning.

I went to my room which had an en suite bathroom and enjoyed a good bath before putting on another new dress. I repaired to what was called the 'coffee room' but was actually a bar where ladies were allowed, unlike the main bar which was for male members only. It was the only annoying thing about the club. I hated being classed as a second-class citizen. As I came by the door, I heard a very American voice saying, "No don't be shy Al, tell us about the fabulous broad who came looking for me today".

Before I could moderate my vulgar behaviour, I shouted, "In England a broad is a freshwater lake, found in Norfolk. In Scotland we call them lochs." I walked on into the hush of the 'coffee room' and ordered a gin and tonic at the bar from Ernest the barman who was an old friend of mine who had served under my father in the Great War. He wanted news of my mother. I could confirm that she was bearing up to the loss of two sons with the help of a French lady of a similar age who had lost her home as a direct result of the war. Ernest was very blunt, but I knew he was kind and had my best interests at heart. He asked, "How are you bearing up Athena?"

I answered, "Ernest to be honest I'm not doing well. The war has scarred me. I grew very fond of a guy who had lost his leg with gangrene. We never were open to each other and then he goes and gets killed flying. Now I just can't reach closure with fighting and killing. I think that it is all I'm good for. I must be good at it, or I would not be alive."

Ernest knew me better than I knew myself. He asked, "Do you really want the war to end?"

I think I was honest when I replied, "Yes I do."

He answered, "I believe you. I think you need to do something heroic to somehow cleanse yourself. You are a beautiful woman. Love will come. The right man will come into your life. It's up to you to keep him alive."

I reached over the bar and squeezed his hand. He added, "I would hate anything to happen to you as I admired your father, so you also need to protect yourself. However, if you get killed like he was through bad luck, maybe that is for the best. I gather there was a unit in the Western Desert who had the motto, 'He who dares wins.' I will put that on your gravestone. Go and get some food in you. Have a good night's sleep. Come back in the bar tomorrow night and tell me how 24 hours has made all the difference."

My father had been mortal, and I had never known him. So, I decided to take another old man's advice. I took my drink through to the dinning room and drunk it with my meal. I vowed to help Rodney French's parents. I even laughed to myself as I got, naked into bed. If Zeus arrived as a swan, he would make a hell of a mess raddling me! I slept well.

I was the first down to breakfast but soon I was joined by none other than Colonel Brad Stevens. He introduced himself. We ate breakfast together. There was no sign of Al. his PA, but Brad had some news for me. He was obviously intrigued by meeting a classy English broad. I was glad I had dressed smartly for breakfast in the club. Brad told me that I was very unlikely to find out anything in London as all the GIs were being demobbed and sent home to the USA. He said that there was indeed a Rodney French who was now a Major who was fighting in the Pacific. He was attached to 75th Infantry Battalion, known as Merrill's Marauders. They were based at Fort Moore which was situated in Columbus Georgia adjacent to Alabama.

Brad told me if I really wanted to find Rodney French, I should hightail myself over to Alabama Airport and take a taxi to Fort Moore. Brad was very helpful. He took me to his office. Al, his PA was instructed to get me on a flight out of Manston in East Kent. He suggested that I travelled light but wore my Wren's officer's uniform. My rank would be a help getting into the USA.

My flight left at 7.00 pm. I returned to the 'Rags Club'. I hastily packed and donned my Naval Uniform and, having left a note behind the bar thanking Ernest for his help got a taxi to Victoria Station. I had time to ring Lily French before I boarded my train to Maidstone East, so that Jack met me at the Station. He was waiting outside as much to my amusement he did not want to waste a penny buying a platform ticket!

I had enjoyable lunch with Jack and Lily. They were pleased that I had made some headway in finding some news as to what had happened to Rodney. I was not actually very hopeful, but I

96

did not want to dampen their enthusiasm. They certainly had not given up hope. This helped me as to carry on and take Ernest's advice. They both insisted on driving me to Manston from Leeds Castle which took under an hour. Jack had been hoarding his petrol coupons. I felt bad but Lily said they had nothing more import than my mission to use them on. They dropped me at the gate of the American airbase. I waved goodbye to them as I walked up to the guard post. I showed the sergeant the letter which Al had prepared and had been signed by Brad. The sergeant asked me to wait as he rang through to the main building. He came off the phone. "They are sending a jeep for you, Mam."

I smiled and thought, 'So far so good so good'.

Both the guys in the guardhouse and the driver of the jeep were intrigued by my arrival. I was very much in a very masculine world. English Broads were obviously linked to good-time girls and easy-lays. I was going to have to overcome these prejudices, not because I was not up for having a good time or for that matter did, I mind being laid. I had put the two months of being a German whore behind me. I had moved on. It was now just something I had had to endure for the sake of my country, like lying in the snow trying to get my revenge on the Germans in the 'Battle of the Bulge'. I still remembered the gentle touch of the young groom in Scotland. I knew that I could enjoy sex again. I hoped I could one day experience deep fulfilling love as a woman and perhaps love for some children as well. First, I had to do something of which I could be really proud, as Ernest had suggested and that was finding out what had happened to Rodney French.

I had a lot to learn first. Brad was a full colonel. This was a pretty senior rank, but I knew there were many more senior who I would have to charm. I hoped I was up to it. At least I wanted to know what had happened to Rodney. It was a genuine desire, not the totally false behaviour in a Gestapo brothel.

The driver parked the jeep in front of the old stately home which was now the home of the HQ of the United States Airforce. (USAF) based at Manston. An officer who introduced himself as Squadron Leader Jack Thompson met me on the steps and said that my case would be delivered to my flight which would be leaving in just over an hour. He kindly took me to the officer's mess for some supper. What I found strange was that I got the feeling that the Americans needed me for something. Sadly, I did not know what it was. However, I was intrigued. I was certain that it was to do with Rodney French. I could not believe it was just to humour his parents or me who they perhaps assumed was his fiancé.

It was a long boring flight and I slept most of the way. There was no alcohol, but I was offered water, sandwiches, tea and biscuits. I was surprised that because of my long sleep I was not affected by the time change. I was whisked through as soon as we landed into the office of an intelligence officer. He did not introduce himself but said he was attached to the 75th Infantry Brigade otherwise know as Merrills Marauders. He asked me, "When did you first meet Rodney French?"

I replied, "In an operation in Arnhem called 'Operation Market Garden'."

He nodded and asked, "We are in communication with a man on a radio on an island in the Pacific south of Japan. He says he is Rodney French. Could you verify him?"

I was dubious, "I don't think that I could confirm his voice on a radio."

The intelligence officer asked, "This is very important. Could you question him to confirm his identity?"

I smiled, "He has seen me naked. I have some cigarette-burn marks on my breasts inflicted by the Gestapo."

He went slightly pale, "You have my sympathy, mam. Please come with me to the communications room."

He led the way to a massive control room. I was introduced to a radio operator called Rick. It was then decided that they would contact Rodney in morse code which they could then encrypt. It seemed as if Rodney, if it was Rodney, had a code and that they knew his fist. Apparently, an operator has a recognisable manner of taping morse which is unique. It now became clear to me. They needed me to check that Rodney had not been captured by the Japanese and was making the transmission under duress having been tortured.

It took some time for Rick to raise Rodney. The intelligence officer and I waited patiently. I wrote down a script which I passed to the intelligence officer. He nodded. At last, they connected to Rodney. Rick started transmitting my script in coded morse.

'What distinctive marks does Athena have?'

'Cigarette-burns.'

'Where?'

'On the underside of her breasts."

'How many burns?'

'Six.'

I started to cry. It had hurt so much, and I had broken down on the sixth cigarette burn. They then got Rodney to relay his message. He was on an Island called Tokuno Shima. This was a granite, volcanic, coral, island in the Amani chain. Its geology was unusual. Rodney had discovered that the Japanese battleship and its escorts was hiding in the atoll.

The intelligence officer seemed pleased and then asked me if I would be prepared to fly to a US Navy carrier group in the pacific. I was not sure whether they did not trust either me or Rodney or indeed either of us. I hoped they did, but they just needed to keep communications open with Rodney.

I had now a long and hazardous journey to get to the carrier in the Pacific which I assumed was heading for Tokuno Shima. The first part of the journey was straight forward but long and tedious. I flew to Hawaii. Then it got very exciting. I was taken in a Vought F4U Corsair out into the pacific to find the carrier group which was destined to attack the Japanese Battleship Yamato and its group of smaller defensive craft. What I did not know was that there were two American submarines on route to the area. I suddenly got spooked by the vastness of the Pacific. I knew that we did not have enough fuel to return to Hawaii. If we did not find the carrier, we would have to ditch in the ocean which certainly did not appeal to me. Why ever had I agreed to help Rodney's parents. I hardly knew the guy and the single time we had met he treated me very badly. I shut my eyes and thought, 'Life is a bitch and then you die. Was this the last day of the war and I was going to die like my father who never saw the fruits of victory leaving my poor mother to grieve over him and her three children. I got a grip on myself. I was not going to die. If need be, I would swim to Tokuno Shimu.'

I started to search the ocean for not just a carrier but a whole carrier fleet. Surely, we should be able to find them. My eyes must have been better than the pilots as it was me who with a sigh of relief saw them and touched his arm and pointed to the left-hand side. That was only the beginning of the drama as we then had to land on the deck of the carrier. It was terrifying but we made it with a gut retching jolt. Mercifully my stomach was empty, so I did not vomit. I was very wobbly as I walked across the deck having jumped down from the cockpit via the wing. I was met by yet another intelligence officer, but he at least introduced him self as Dick Roberts. He took me immediately to meet the captain who was in conversation with the admiral on the bridge.

He did his best to appear to be friendly and reassuring, "Your limey fiancé has been most helpful in locating the Yamato. We are most grateful to you for coming out here to verify that my airman will not be flying into a trap. We once again need you to check that he has not been captured by the enemy."

The admiral added his two-penny worth, "I need you back here to eyeball me before I risk American lives. Get to it."

I did not reply but just saluted before I turned about and followed Dick to the radio room. When we were out of earshot, I asked him if the Admiral was always that abrupt. Dick said he normally was very relaxed, but this attack was being forced on him by the top brass in the United States. I just hoped that I was not going to be used as a pawn in a power play.

It seemed to take forever for them in the radio room to contact Rodney. He confirmed that all the Japanese flotilla was still in Tokuno Shimu harbour but that he had seen two more anti-aircraft positions placed to the south of the harbour. I was happy that Rodney was not transmitting under duress when he described in detail how he had made me kill the two German lookouts in the electricity relay tower near to the bridge south of Arnhem in the nude. Dick's face was a study when he heard this information. He asked, "Is he really your fiancé?" I had to admit that he wasn't but that was the only way I could get any information for his parents as to whether he was still alive as he had been reported, 'missing believed dead'.

Dick shook his head, "I hope for everyone's sake we can get him out alive. He sounds a real bastard, but he certainly is a brave guy".

I replied, "He was awarded a VC after Arnhem. The guys who get those are pretty special."

Dick answered, "I know".

Then we were on our way back to see the admiral. He upstaged me by being considerably more friendly, "I have been shown a copy of your file. You are an unusual young woman. Can you verify the information?"

I answered, "I can, Sir. I am sorry that your airmen will encounter tougher opposition."

He shrugged, "I therefore have a job for you. I want you to use your shooting skills as a sniper to take those two new positions out. It needs to be a totally synchronised operation as it is imperative that the Japanese do not suspect that we are coming. You will start firing only when you hear the arrival of our aircraft. Is that understood?"

I replied, "Yes Sir."

The admiral turned to the captain, "Ted, I am giving you the green light. Dick, kindly brief this allied officer and get her in position to do a good job." The admiral then strode off the bridge to a shocked silence. Dick recovered quickly, "Athena I have a helicopter standing by to deliver you and your rifle to a submarine. The submarine will put you ashore on Tokuno Shimu tonight. The aircraft raid is planned for dawn tomorrow."

That was it. This time the pilot and me had to locate a submarine, but least it was only sixty miles away. I was going to be dropped from a two-seater Sikorsky R-4 helicopter. We had to be quick as it was going to be dark in two hours and the helicopter had to get back in daylight. I was just thankful that I was not going to be parachuted in. I was issued with a Lise Carbine and some ammunition, and we were off. The pilot was pleased that I was light as he could take some extra fuel in a drop tank. It was an amazing journey skimming across the waves. His navigation was spot on and within forty minutes I was jumping out on to the deck of a submarine. It was already diving by the time I was climbing down the rungs of the ladder in the control tower.

I was a surprise. They had not expected a woman. Mercifully they had a small wet suit which fitted me. The crew found me a novelty and I was well fed before being allowed six hours sleep. They dropped me fifty yards from the beach at periscope depth and I had a hard swim with my rifle and ammunition. They promised to pick me up again the following night at 2.00 am.

I was lucky there was very little wind and I got ashore without any problems. I had to climb up on to a ridge which would overlook the anti-aircraft nests. I wondered where Rodney was. I did not want to run into him in the dark. Obviously, it was vital that I did not forewarn the Japanese sentries. I hoped that they were not on full alert as they were so far from the American island-hopping advance.

My years of training behind German lines helped me but all the same this climb was very hard work and very scary. At one stage I thought I was not going to make it before dawn but mercifully I had gone quicker that I imagined. I was terrified of letting down the admiral. I suppose being in such a remote position in charge of so many lives would make anyone bad tempered. He had only seemed happy when he had sent me on an impossibly dangerous mission and had made the decision to attack.

There was still no glimmer of light of the dawn on my right as I reached the crest of the ridge. I lay waiting and listening. I think it was the sound of a rifle being grounded which alerted me to the position of the two lookouts. They must have been patrolling and reached the end of their beat, as I then heard them talking.

I moved stealthily down the ten feet to the path which joined the two lookouts. I waited and then I heard a man coming towards me. He made quite a noise, and it was easy for me to follow him for fifty yards or so before I closed behind him and noiselessly cut his throat, as I had learnt in France in what felt like a lifetime ago. Now I had the harder job to backtrack and find the other enemy. I felt it was vital that I was not overlooked when I took up a sniping position.

Killing the second man was a mission and I was not nearly as quiet as I would have liked. The goddess of war was kind, and the noise did not appear to alert any further sentries down the picket line. In the gloom I perceived a large rock about fifteen feet inland, below the path. I made my way down to it and found that it would be a suitable place for me to use for my covert shooting. I had passed several large rocks which would give me some cover when I needed to make my escape.

I scanned the slope below me, but I could not see the anti-aircraft guns. I hunkered down and just had to wait. I knew that I would only have a few minutes to identify my targets and eliminate them before the vulnerable American planes would arrive. They would be targets, not only for these shore-based guns but also for all the guns on the boats which I could just make out in the harbour.

I had some luck. I spied a brief glimpse of a light down the slope. I decided to concentrate on that and leave the second position for later when the dawn came. I hoped that I could adjust the sights of my carbine with only two shots. It was vital that I killed the gunners before they got shooting at the planes. I hoped they would not have any marksmen. They obviously would not expect one to be up above them. They would not be aware of Rodney. He must have been very careful to stay hidden.

Then I heard the noise of a plane. Dick Roberts had told me that when I heard the noise it would mean that the first plane was still ten minutes away. Would the dawn come to help me? I waited. Were the enemy alerted? Hopefully they would think the noise was from Japanese Zeros. It got lighter. There was still no movement from the anti-aircraft units. The ships were quiet. Was this going to be a small pay-back for Pearl Harbour?

Now I could see movement through my scope. I hoped my sights were not too off centre. I saw a torso of a man washing his face in a bucket. I fired. I hit the bucket. My sights were slightly sighted to the right. I adjusted them and now I could see a large amount of activity. I aimed and hit one man, then another. They made no effort to find cover. I hit all four men before I had to change magazines. I started to search for the second gun. I found it about two hundred yards away. They must have become aware that enemy planes were about to attack. The noise certainly was much lounder. I hit a man who was just fitting the belt to the heavy machine gun. I aimed at the gun as there were no human targets. I was lucky as I must have hit the mechanism. Hopefully

I had jammed it. Now the USAF was in action. There were massive explosions on board the ships. What was much more relevant for me was that I had incoming small-arms fire. I had been spotted. I had done enough. It was time to exit the scene. I started making my way quickly up through the rocks. I was hit on the face by a rock splinter which made me fall. There was a lot of blood but no real damage. It was just a flesh wound. I got up and kept going. I did not stop until I was over the sentry's path and then over the ridge. The blood was annoying as I would be leaving a trail which even a child could follow. Stealth was not needed now. I needed to get out of the area as quickly as possible.

Because I was athletic, I bounded down the volcanic ridge which as it was mainly scree allowed me to take enormous leaps and land sliding on my bottom. As soon as I reached the beach I waded into the surf and with my rifle on my back I set off swimming out to some rocks which were on the side of the little cove. I swam around the rocks to the seaward side and found a hiding place in them.

I took stock of the situation. As there was a small overhang I could rest up in the shade. I had my water bottle. I planned to remain there until the submarine arrived. I stayed undiscovered during the heat of the day. I hoped that the Japanese had enough to keep them occupied with rescuing survivors from the attack on the fleet. I was pleased that the US Admiral obviously thought I had done a good job in dealing with the anti-aircraft defences as he sent in another attack early in the afternoon. I could see the aircraft circling and I could hear the bombardment. I hoped the US Army had plans to land on the island as the war progressed. Now I hoped the US Navy would remember to take me off the island and back to the carrier.

Chapter 10

It was dusk and I was getting tired and thirsty, as I had to ration my water. I was also hungry, but I knew I just had to man up and wait for my rescuers. The Japanese had other ideas. Using the scope on my rifle I watched a cameo of five years ago on the beaches of France repeated here on Tokuno Shimu. Two Japanese soldiers were driving a man along the beach with their rifle buts. When he fell down, they kicked him. To my horror it was Rodney French. I did not hesitate. I shot them both with two easy shots as I was only about two hundred yards away.

I slung my rifle on back and set off swimming as fast I could to the beach. By the time I got to him, Rodney was on his feet and was dragging one of his dead captors out into the surf. He did not know what had happened, but he knew that someone had shot them. He did not want other Japanese soldiers to find the bodies. He recognised me immediately, "Oh my god, what the hell are you doing here? Help me drag these bodies out of sight."

I said nothing but just did what I was told. It was much easier with two of us and we soon had the bodies hidden behind some rocks and covered by rocks and sand. We were lucky the tide was coming in and they would be covered very soon. We swept the sand with palm fonds as well as we could on the beach to hide the incident. We hoped it would allow our escape undetected. Rodney threw one of the Japanese rifles far out into the deep water. He slung the other together with an ammunition belt on his back. We both took a water bottle and set off swimming out to the rocks. Because the tide had come in it seemed a long way, but we made it. It was a good hiding place and was getting better all the time as the tide was coming in. I hoped that the Japanese would not have a patrol boat out going around the island. I thought it was extremely unlikely, as I was certain any small boats would be busy rescuing Japanese sailors off the sinking vessels in the bay on the other side of the ridge.

We had a lot of catching up to do. Rodney kept firing questions at me. The only way I could stop him was by saying he was worse that the Gestapo. I did manage to find out why the British Government thought he was missing believed dead. It was because the Americans had sent him on this secret mission, and they did not trust the British not to let on to any other source and thereby alert the Japanese. It explained why the Americans had at first given me the run around in London. He was highly amused that I had pretended to be his fiancé. He made a very dry comment, "Why ever would I propose to you?"

I retorted, "I have just saved your life!"

He replied, "Only as an afterthought. You were going to leave the island. I did not feature on your radar."

I had to admit he was right. Somehow, we deserved each other we were both selfish, overconfident bastards. Our only redeeming feature was that we both were brave and proud to serve our country. Rodney did admit he was gobsmacked when I had come on the radio. He had been dropped on Tokuno Shimu with a radio by a submarine which had then been deployed out of that theatre of the Pacific. He knew the island well since his gap-year days and so like me in France had managed to stay hidden for several months. He had only broken radio silence when the Yamato battleship and its fleet had arrived.

I asked him, "Have you been lonely?"

He replied, "No I like my own company."

I nodded, "I was the same when I was hiding alone in France."

He asked, "Did you really pretend to be my fiancé or was it wishful thinking?"

I retorted, "It certainly wasn't. You are totally impossible. You have such an enormous ego. Whatever makes you think I want to be married to you?"

He replied, "Would it surprise you to learn that not a day has gone by since Arnhem when I have not thought about you."

I looked at him in amazement. I was amazed by his admission. We sat in silence just looking at each other as the sun set. I was happy to cuddle in his arms for our long chilly wait until 2.00 am. Rodney told me of his capture. He had been picked up by the two men purely by bad luck. He thought they were deserters who had just chanced to decide to hide in the cave with its tiny entrance where he had been hiding. He had been asleep, and they had surprised him. He thought they planned to hand him over to their superiors to curry favour. He said that they talked very little, and he could not understand their Japanese. I asked about the radio. He said that would not be a problem even if it should be found in its separate hiding place, as it had a self-destruct mechanism so that unless the correct code was used it blew up, so that it was unusable.

After midnight we both were finding it difficult to stay awake, so we told each other stories about what we had experienced during the war. Rodney was interested in James. I could not really explain my strange relationship with him. Rodney could not understand how we had never had sex. I could not understand why not either. I suggested it was because I had nursed him for so long. Rodney certainly woke me up when he said, "I will just have to make sure you never nurse me anytime."

It confirmed that he wanted to have sex with me in spite of the fact that we always seemed to be at cross purposes and rubbed each other up the wrong way. I wondered if we would be different in peacetime when life would be more relaxed. I doubted if it would be.

At last, I spotted the periscope of the submarine. It came to within thirty yards of us, so it was an easy swim. We both kept our weapons. It was the same submarine which had dropped me off but of course the crew did not know or expect Rodney. I was greatly relieved to be submerged and heading well away from the enemy. I was longing for a shower and a good hair wash. Instead, I had to suffer the smell of forty men. At least Rodney had only smelt of sea water.

We travelled on the surface so the main engines powered by diesel could recharge the batteries. The look out in the conning-tower spotted an enemy aircraft so we had to dive halfway through the morning. The plane must have radioed our position as we were soon the target for depth charges from two Japanese destroyers. We all had to cling on to something solid as every explosion resulted in severe rocking. I clung on to Rodney which he seemed to relish. It was a truly harrowing experience we descended to three hundred feet and then went silent, and the destroyers mercifully seemed to lose us. In fact, what we did not know was that the US Marines had landed on the strategic Japanese island of Okinawa. Our carrier had been sent to support the landings and therefore we were sailing to point in the ocean which was no longer a haven. We were very much on our own. When we eventually contacted Hawaii, we were routed to rendezvous with a support ship to refuel. This did not have a helicopter and so we were ordered to stay on board the submarine and help protect the fleet standing off Okinawa below the skyline, where a major battle was in process.

So, no shower, no hair wash. I had got use to the smell. Rodney and I stank just as badly. We were allowed out on the very small deck of the submarine in relays at night when we were on the surface. Rodney and I exercised together. The rest of the time we were bottled up in the submarine with the crew. I found this a strange and a very annoying experience. Rodney obviously felt the same. This in a strange way brought us closer together. We both wanted sex but even as a supposed engaged couple that was not possible. This added to our frustration. Therefore, when we were summoned ashore on to Okinawa as a sniper team, we were happy to go along.

We were dropped by a rubber dingy on a beach held by the Americans who were trying desperately to dislodge the Japanese who were fighting to the death to defend the island which was part of their country. They had had plenty of time to prepare their defences.

I was the sniper and Rodney was designated as my spotter a task which he did not relish. I also did not want him as a spotter as I had never had one before. So, to keep the peace he came as my guard. This was helpful. I was much more relaxed particularly when we were close to the enemy knowing that Rodney had my back. He was also helpful in the shower to protect me from the GIs who thought a limey broad was fair game. My mood did change after a shower and some better food.

We climbed up to the front line and set about our task. This was extremely difficult. The enemy were very well protected, and they had snipers of their own. Rodney had a periscope so that he could survey the target area without any risk. However, they also had periscopes. It was just too dangerous to show oneself. We returned from the front line without any success. This did not suit our British pride and so Rodney and I decided to see if we could get closer to the enemy's defences. I would continue to use my rifle, but Rodney would carry a grenade launcher. The American sergeant at arms wisely issued us with Colt 45s as side arms. This saved our lives as we were attacked at dusk by a four-man Japanese patrol. The Colt is a very handy weapon with a devastating power to, not only kill one's attacker, but also to wound enough to prevent retaliation. We survived but both suffered deep flesh wounds which needed surgery. We were operated on in a field hospital on the island and then we were transferred off the island to a hospital boat. My wound was in my arm and healed quickly. Rodney was hit in the thigh. The bullet missed the femur but resulted in severe sepsis. It looked at one stage as if he was going to lose his leg. His salvation was the provision of a new antibacterial wonder drug called a sulphonamide. At one point I thought I was yet again destined to lose a one-legged man who I now realised that I loved.

We were returning across the Pacific to San Francisco when the Americans dropped the two nuclear bombs, The first on the 6th of August 1945 on Hiroshima and the second on the 9th of August on Nagasaki. I was very relieved when we were told in San Francisco on the 14th of August that the Japanese had surrendered.

We both had survived. We managed to get word to our respective families. I knew my mother would still be sad about the loss of her sons but at least she might have the chance of some grandchildren. I had kept my word to Rodney's parents. I had found him for them and would bring him home.

About the Author

Graham Duncanson

I was born on a farm in 1944. I learnt to read at a local school but found it difficult. Mathematics on the other hand was very easy. I dreaded school work exercises like 'what was the most interesting thing that you did in the holidays'. I failed 'O' level English Language the first time around but passed English Literature.

I am a compulsive traveller. At five years of age I set my sights on Africa. Animals interested me, particularly farm and game animals. I spend a considerable amount of time with our elderly shepherd, Harry Weller, who was a very patient teacher. Other than my mother, he was the only person to cry, when having completed my veterinary degree at Bristol Veterinary School, I took up a post in Kenya. There was no TV. I read a large amount. After eight years I returned to the UK and joined a practice in Norfolk where I have been ever since. I got married to Jane. Sadly our marriage only lasted twenty years but resulted in a son Henry an economist and a daughter Amelia a veterinary surgeon.

I have always been interested in disseminating knowledge and so I published in peer reviewed journals and wrote articles in veterinary newspapers. My doctorate asked the question, 'Does the veterinary profession need another peer reviewed journal?' History has agreed with my conclusion that it doesn't, only an improvement in the existing journals.

To find out more about Graham and his books:

Facebook - https://www.facebook.com/graham.duncanson.7

LinkedIn - http://linkedin.com/in/graham-duncanson-8624105b

All my novels are available from Amazon under GRAHAM DUNCANSON.

Mating Lions by Graham Duncanson

In 1966 Jim Scott, aged 22, qualifies as a veterinary surgeon and lands the job of his dreams working in Kenya. Arriving in Kenya and knowing no one, he quickly makes friends.

His work involves travelling in the arid areas of Northern Kenya, carrying out a wide variety of veterinary jobs, as well as doing some clandestine spying for the British Government.

After a girl that he is fond of returns to England, he decides to learn to fly. This leads him into a seriously dangerous mission requested by his controller, the wife of the High Commissioner. When they eventually meet at a reception at the High Commission, it's a case of love at first sight. They go clandestinely together at day break to Nairobi Game Park and they are lucky to see two lions mating.

Their torrid affair ends in tragedy. Jim survives, but will he be mentally as well as physically scarred for life?

This is the first book of a trilogy.

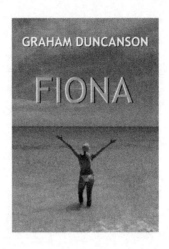

Fiona by Graham Duncanson

In 1966 Jim Scott, aged 22, qualified as a veterinary surgeon and landed the job of his dreams working in Kenya. Just before leaving, he fell in love with Fiona, a Scottish girl, but there was no chance of a lasting relationship and they agreed to part.

Three and a half years later, Jim is mentally and physically scarred by a lion, which he kills with a '*panga*', but not before it kills a woman he cares about.

At his wit's end working through the tragedy, Fiona comes out to Kenya. They find their love has not died, but Jim is too hung up on the past. Fi takes the lead and loves his fears away and they start planning a wedding and a family and their lives together.

Then, persuaded by a senior MI6 officer to gather information on their travels in Kenya and in other African countries, they face danger that could threaten everything they've worked for and dreamed of.

Fiona is book two of the Mating Lions Trilogy.

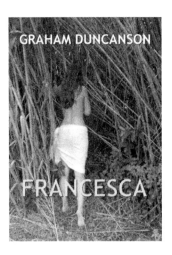

Francesca by Graham Duncanson

In 1939 in Northern Kenya, after an unpleasant incident with a German, a young Italian girl decides to throw in her lot with a young District Officer, Jack Harding.

She is actually half-English, and when her language skills are discovered by the Kenyan authorities, she and Jack, with the help of a group of Rendile tribesmen, thwart an attack by the Italians. During their adventures, the relationship between Francesca and Jack grows.

Jack enlists to fight the war and is rapidly promoted and posted to Burma, where he is captured by the Japanese and imprisoned in a POW camp.

Meanwhile, Francesca, who hates school in Nairobi and is expelled, turns his large house into a successful hotel.

She is summoned to London in 1946 by Sir Richard Harding as Jack, his youngest son, has now been declared, 'Missing believed dead'.

Francesca convinces Sir Richard that Jack may still be alive and she travels to Burma determined to try to find him.

GRAHAM DUNCANSON

ANNA

Anna by Graham Duncanson

Anna is fourteen. She foolishly tries to rescues a zebra foal from a crocodile in Kenya. Her life is saved by a vet in his twenties who thinks she is in her gap year.

He takes her on a flight to watch him play rugby. She kisses him after the game, but she then has to return to the UK. Anna develops a passion for rugby and a determination to become a vet.

Four years later she comes to Kenya to find him. They travel in an old Landrover, overland through Europe and fall in love but there is a long road before them before they can hope to get married.

Katie by Graham Duncanson

It is 1964. Katie is eighteen and has trained to be an air hostess. She has just completed her first long haul flight to Kenya. Because of scheduling difficulties, the whole crew have been granted a seven night stopover and they decide to go on a minibus safari around the game parks.

Katie strongly resists the totally inappropriate advances of the senior captain and so he blocks her inclusion on the safari.

Left on her own, she meets Ian, a vet who is twelve years older than her. He appears to be kind and offers to take her on a really exciting safari to Northern Kenya. Their relationship develops and leads to some exciting escapades which would certainly have broken a weaker girl, both physically and mentally. Then Ian gets arrested on a trip to Iran. Katie requires all her fortitude to attempt a rescue.

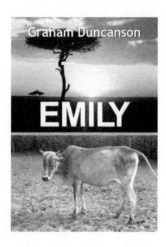

Emily by Graham Duncanson

Emily is a farmer's daughter who had a passion to become a veterinary surgeon and go to work in Africa. She qualifies only to find that her small stature and her feminine good looks are against her. She is unable to secure employment.

She gets a break when her great aunt asks her to come out to Kenya and help her run her large ranch in the Northern Frontier District. Getting to the ranch is not easy. However her great aunt is very welcoming. Emily's world disintegrates around her when her great aunt dies during her first night on the ranch. She is befriended by Simon, a young, but more senior vet, who goes out of his way to help her. She falls in love with him, but he keeps her at arm's length.

Emily shows courage and fortitude. She gains respect not only from her employees on the ranch but also from the senior members of the Veterinary Department and the Government Administration.

She meets Simon's family and gains an insight into his character, but is this sufficient to earn his love?

Polly by Graham Duncanson

Polly is eighteen, when her father, a professional hunter, is killed by a wounded buffalo. Her mother died when she was born. In theory she is totally on her own. However, the Kenyans, who worked for her father and have known her all her life, are very loyal. She is determined to keep the business afloat to protect their jobs. Kenya has recently become independent and there is large scale unemployment.

When she finds out that her father had borrowed heavily from the bank and they are going to close the business down and make her bankrupt, she does not despair. She even considers selling herself to a wealthy rancher.

Will her beautiful smile and wonderful figure be enough for her to marry the older man she really loves?

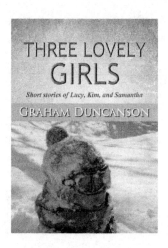

Three Lovely Girls by Graham Duncanson

Three short stories about three lovely girls in very different circumstances who fall in love.

It's Lucy's sixteenth birthday. She can never please her mother. She tries but somehow they are not on the same wavelength. A random meeting at the top of a ski run on Christmas Day leads her to a very exciting week, much to her mother's disapproval. Lucy despairs that her mother will never accept her new boyfriend.

Kim is totally fed up with her young stepmother. She decides to run away. Not a simple task as her father is the President of the USA. Help comes in the form of an old veterinary surgeon. Will they both escape and allow Kim to follow her dream.

Samantha is at her wits end. She is all alone in Norfolk just before Christmas. A chance meeting at the top of a church tower results in a job in a ski resort and an epic flight in a small plane to Kenya may cause more problems than it solves.

122

Lucy by Graham Duncanson

It's Lucy's sixteenth birthday. A random meeting at the top of a ski run on Christmas Day leads to a fast moving love affair. Her mother finds out that Lucy has spent the last night of the holiday with Peter. She calls Lucy a harlot and says she will never speak to her again. Her father normally takes Lucy's side but he fails to calm down his wife.

Lucy runs away from home to Scotland, mainly to save her parent's marriage. She learns to look after sheep, having rescued an elderly shepherd. She is very happy living with him and makes many, new friends. Her life takes a very rapid movement upwards after she rescues Lord Carmichael, Peter's grandfather from a car accident in a deep, cold, Scottish river. The question is, '*Will this lead her back to Peter*'?

The first chapter of *Lucy* was previously published as a short story in *Three Lovely Girls*.

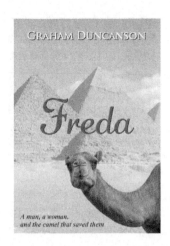

Freda by Graham Duncanson

Set in the time of the 2017 Churchill film, *Darkest Hour*, we follow Gordon, a young British Officer in the King's African Rifles in 1939. He is sent off alone to try and gain intelligence for British Army on the possible Italian invasion of Kenya. He links up with Emma, Lord Wakefield's daughter who is half Italian. They experience some horrendous escapades with a camel called Freda, and fall in love. They get involved in the hostilities in the Western Desert. The chances of their survival appear to be remote. Can their love and courage save Cairo from the Axis Powers?

Jenny by Graham Duncanson

Jenny is a newly qualified vet who having been a bit of a party girl at Cambridge has not achieved the academic results her professor would have wished. He is reluctant to pass her on her resit results. Jenny is offered a way into the profession by agreeing to go to work in Kenya, where they are desperate for field veterinarians. Jenny has always loved adventures and so going to Africa really appeals to her. She finds herself totally on her own in Mombasa on Christmas Eve.

Men, particularly older men, find her very attractive. On the whole they go out of their way to help her. However, she finds herself in a very challenging situation and has no one available to guide her. Her courage does not desert her and she copes admirably. She meets a pilot called Matt and they become very close friends, but sadly their relationship is going to be very short. Jenny is left alone and has to rely on her fortitude to get her out of a very dark place.

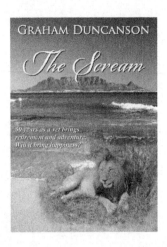

The Scream by Graham Duncanson

Jim Scott is a veterinary surgeon who worked in Kenya, having qualified in 1966. His early career is described in 'Mating Lions' and 'Fiona'. Fiona, the love of his life, dies of cancer in 2012.

He continues to practice in the UK, but his clandestine past catches up with him. He decides to set off on a bicycle ride from his home in Norfolk to Cape Town. He has many different companions riding with him in a relay to keep him company, including his five daughters.

After a logistical problem in Northern Kenya, he is on his own, when he faces the most dangerous part, not only of this journey, but also of his life.

This is the final book in the Mating Lions Trilogy.

Sarah by Graham Duncanson

As a very young girl, Sarah set her sights on Hector, who is ten years her senior. When he leaves Kenya aged eighteen to go to England to study to be a vet, she plucks up courage to kiss him.

By the time he returns she is much more mature and has her flying license. Their love quickly blossoms, but it is 1938 and war threatens everything. They know that they will have to part, but they take a giant leap of faith and get married.

Separately they face horrendous dangers. Their heroic efforts for the allied cause do not go unnoticed. Will Sarah's strength and fortitude save them both in the end?

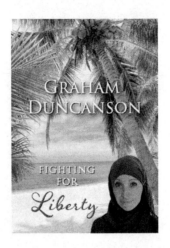

Fighting for Liberty by Graham Duncanson

Libby is a newly qualified secret agent. On her first assignment she meets a retired agent who is three times her age, Jim Scott. There is an instant bond between them. They are thrown together trying to discover the traitor in their ranks. She learns a lot from him. It is only when she is alone without him that she realises how deeply she was in love with him. The story is an adventure of survival. Will she be able to put the past behind her and reach closure?

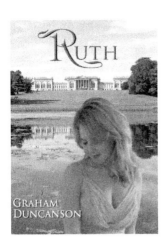

Ruth by Graham Duncanson

This is a rags to riches romance. Ruth, the heroine, was the daughter of a whore attached to The Duke of Wellington's Peninsular Army. She thinks that she was born in 1800. She hardly remembers her mother who died when she was only five years old. She follows the British army to Waterloo where she steals a horse and rescues a young, blinded, cavalry officer, who actually is Lord Chandos. They fall in love and with her help they arrive at his country seat, 'Stowe'. She bears him ten children who all play major roles in the story. Her mission is to help him to regain his sight.

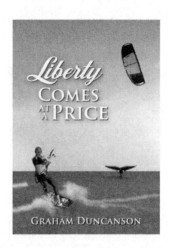

Liberty Comes at a Price by Graham Duncanson

This is a stand alone novel but it does follow my previous novel 'Fighting for Liberty'.

Libby and her three colleagues, Kate, Rosemary and Gemma are given their most dangerous assignment to date. They carry out their task with ruthless efficiency. Other assignments follow until disaster strikes. Libby is left sad and alone. A man comes on to her radar, but they are not destined to make a life together. Will happiness always allude her?

The Sinners by Graham Duncanson

Two young Victorian teenagers in aristocratic Scotland fall in love, only to find out that they can never marry as they both have the same father. Far from feeling repugnance for each other, they can not stem their physical attraction. They strive to behave in society as brother and sister. In private they are sinners. They make an escape to East Africa where their liberal behaviour is tolerated rather than welcomed. They rescue some slaves and climb Mount Kilimanjaro. Only when they reach Voi in Kenya and The Great War is finished do they find real happiness.

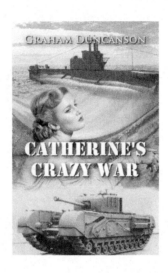

Catherine's Crazy War by Graham Duncanson

One of Britain's spymasters, Bertie who is in his forties has been lusting after Catherine since he caught her swimming in the nude when she was sixteen.

Catherine is driven by the three Ps. She is patriotic, passionate and promiscuous. Bertie is happy to take her virginity on her request on her eighteenth birthday, the day when Britain declared war on Nazi Germany. She saves him from a certain assassination attempt. A bond is forged between them which all the dark aspects of war can not break.

The chances of either of them surviving the war are slight. The risks they are taking for their country are enormous and are requested at the highest level, not only in bomb torn London but also in many other theatres of the conflict.

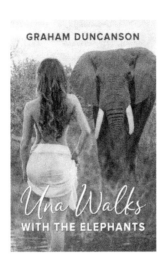

GRAHAM DUNCANSON

Una Walks With The Elephants by Graham Duncanson

Una is a patriot. This is her diary. She uses her many talents to serve her country in The First World War. Her courage shines through in the mainly male dominated war.

First and foremost she was a nurse on the Western Front. Here she also learnt to tunnel with Welsh miners before becoming a sniper using her superb eyesight and terrifying accuracy with a rifle. Thus she was a natural with a Lewis gun in the primitive aircraft of the Royal Flying Corps. She becomes a pilot and destroys a Zeppelin over London Docks.

She meets her future husband, Ronald Nesbitt and they, as a duo, attempt to destroy the Turkish rail network in the Middle East. Tragically he dies in her arms.

She is lucky and is rescued by a Sheik before The British Military Intelligence require her services. The chances of her survival is remote after she sets off on a secret mission to East Africa.

Una's Second War by Graham Duncanson

Una's husband died in 'The Great War' in her arms. She meets James Robertson in the bush in Africa. She saves his life and without informing him selects him to be her second husband. She helps him to develop a very successful ranch in Kenya with the help of two African friends. She bears him three daughters.

James is captured at Dunkirk. Una needs the help of her youngest daughter. Their skills as aviators are required to effect his rescue. The whole family can then focus on, not only defeating the Nazis, but also exposing their heinous crimes against humanity.

GRAHAM DUNCANSON

SAVING *Lydia*

Saving Lydia by Graham Duncanson

This is a love story between a young destitute publisher, Lydia and an old retired vet, Dick. It is set in the time of the Covid Pandemic. There is a very large age gap between them. Lydia is very depressed and Dick is lonely. However something sparks between them. They are in fact ideally suited as Dick is very sympathetic and understanding. He is a benevolent father figure which Lydia needs. They become very close as they are locked down together. Lydia actually is very adventurous and outward going. With his help she blossoms and her wicked sense of humour comes to the fore. They are reported to the police for committing incest and indecent behaviour. This is clearly seen as rubbish by the investigating police officers, who become their friends.

Dick teaches Lydia all about veterinary practice both in England and in Kenya. She appreciates his passion for flying and for rugby football. Dick's past catches up with him. Lydia does not hesitate to stand by him. They make a formidable pair.

Sylvie by Graham Duncanson

Sylvie is a French girl who has to endure the murder of her parents by the Gestapo on the day before D Day. She saves the lives of a British tank crew and manages to stay with them, when they are part of the force which liberates Paris. Disaster strikes when their squadron attempts to link up with the besieged parachute regiments who have been dropped on Arnhem. She nurses the tank squadron commander after she has rescued him, when he has been crushed by his tank. At the end of the war he is demobbed to England and he brings her with him. It is only then that she really becomes aware of his wealth and aristocratic origins.

Afsoon by Graham Duncanson

Afsoon escapes the Taliban in August 2021 having seen them murder her family. She escapes in the wheel arch of a transport plane and is found dying at Brize Norton. She survives and is befriended by an old dairy farmer who not only adopts her, but also teaches her to play cricket. She is passionate in her desire to be British. Her intelligence and her ability to play cricket enable her to get a place at Cambridge Veterinary School to read Veterinary Science. Her bravery and resilience insure her survival in a dangerous world. Will her courage and ability to reflect on her past lead her to a happy life?

Emma by Graham Duncanson

Emma was at home at the outbreak of the Second World War. She had received acceptance to go up to Oxford to read mathematics in a month's time. That was not to be. With the help of the security services, she was recruited by the RAF for a crucial role. The bait was that she was going to be trained to fight. That does not stop her falling in love.

Annabel's Vow by Graham Duncanson

A chance meeting by Annabel and Tom in a centre collecting first aid equipment for Ukraine in Norwich leads to a hair-raising trip in a transit van to Ukraine. This hardens Annabel's resolve to help the Ukrainian army to defeat the Russian invaders. The two become a formidable duo and have many successes.

Annabel is very circumspect in what she tells her parents. Her mother finds no problems with her spending her gap year in helping Ukrainian refugees. Little does her mother know that Annabel helps Tom and his associates to drop a bomb on the Russian command centre in Mariupol. Luck runs out for Tom who is killed. Annabel plans revenge.

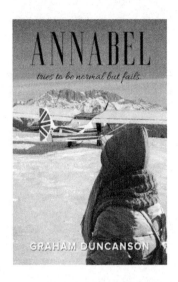

Annabel Tries to Be Normal but Fails by Graham Duncanson

After a rather violent second half of her gap year, Annabel settles down at Oxford. However hard she tries she cannot seem to have a normal life. She is far from an average student as she learns to fly and falls in love with yet another man much older than herself. He like her is a skier. They have good times together on the slopes and on a holiday to Kenya. Then her world seems to crumble when he gets killed flying a light aircraft. Will she ever find lasting happiness?

Frostie Talks in the Shower by Graham Duncanson

Frostie and Richard meet in November 2022. They are both independent in their late twenties. They are brought together by a dog, Ruth, who is very special. She has been trained to guide blind people. Richard had been blinded while in the army on a special operation. Now he has left the army having been trained as a financial adviser.

There is an obvious attraction between them, but their professional careers raised many difficulties. Neither of them knew whether these problems were insurmountable. Would their time and adventures, together and apart, bring about more than just a friendship?

That's No Place for a Girl by Graham Duncanson

My name is Tanya. I am a practicing rural vet, a generation behind James Herriot before his books have been published or shown on television. I have two problems; I am small in stature and said to be very pretty. The men who I deal with, do not take me seriously. I have many useful attributes; For my size I am physically strong, I have a wicked sense of humour, I like men of all ages, I am not shy, I am a good linguist and I am constantly reflecting on my life. This is the story of my early career.

Printed in Great Britain
by Amazon

29649659R00086